the days of

Bluegrass Love

the days of

EDWARD VAN DE VENDEL

Translated by EMMA RAULT

LQ

LEVINE QUERIDO

Montclair · Amsterdam · Hoboken

This is an Em Querido book

Published by Levine Querido

LQ

LEVINE QUERIDO

www.levinequerido.com • info@levinequerido.com

Levine Querido is distributed by Chronicle Books LLC

Copyright © 1999 by Edward van de Vendel

Translation © 2022 by Emma Rault

Originally published in the Netherlands by Querido NL

All rights reserved

Library of Congress Control Number: 2020937518

ISBN 978-1-64614-046-6

Printed and bound in China

Published May 2022

First printing

This publication has been made possible with financial
support from the Dutch Foundation for Literature.

N ederlands
letterenfonds
dutch foundation
for literature

"We're good friends, and it's good to be . . . you know . . . good friends. That's a good thing . . ."

River Phoenix in *My Own Private Idaho*

Summer 1999

First Half

TYCHO HAD NEVER BEEN on a plane—but he'd experienced a moon landing, live and up close.

I N THE ORCHARD WHERE he'd been working to save up money for his ticket, he'd met Nina. After a day of thinning plums, she'd coaxed him to her house and to her bedroom. They'd sat down on her bed: Nina was laughing, Tycho was talking over her, and then she'd started fumbling with the buttons of his shirt. Slowly unfastening them, from top to bottom—as if counting down to zero, as if pulling the petals off a flower . . .

Tycho let the sleeves slide off his arms. His shirt fell helplessly to the floor. Nina grabbed the hem of Tycho's undershirt and pulled on it. He held his hands up and said, "Help!" Nina giggled—and took her top off. They fell back onto the bed and gently turned, their bellies touching. He could feel Nina breathing as she guided his hands to her bra clasp. He fumbled with it. She kissed him. Then she lifted herself up on her elbow, allowing him to pull the bra from between them. She arched her back and her breasts touched against his skin. For the first time, he felt that double pressure of velvet on his smooth body. Like the legs of a lunar module, carefully touching down. Nineteen sixty-nine, Tycho thought. First man on the moon . . .

W HEN HE BIKED HOME that evening, the night wasn't blue, but pale—like skin.

Yes, the moon was glowing, as pale as Nina's skin.

For years Tycho had lived in his pencil case. His days had opened and shut like his schoolbooks. He was the faceless pupil, the son whose parents each recognized half of themselves in him. He looked in the mirror twice a day—once in the morning, and once in the evening—and during the hours in between he didn't think about himself.

Until his senior year. That's when everyone started asking him what he intended to study. What his plans for the future were. Whether he was moving out, to the city. For a while he replied, "Oh jeez, I don't know," but one afternoon he sat down, opened his computer, and typed his name forty times in a row. Tycho Zeling. Tycho Zeling. Tycho Zeling.

Then he ran to the bathroom to look in the mirror. He saw the startled expression in his eyes. He thought his nose was too small, his lips too full, and his short blond hair too lifeless, as if someone had dropped it on his head by accident. He decided to buy stronger hair gel, take a trip to America, and go a year without thinking about college.

His parents said "What?" and "Oh" and nodded cautiously.

I N THE RESTROOM AT the airport, Tycho checked the mirror to see if his hair was mussed up nicely. It was just as it should be. It had to be sticking up in different directions, like signposts pointing his busy mind toward all the corners of the world. He ran a hand through it and headed off to pee.

Men are hunters, he thought, or there wouldn't be pictures of flies in these urinals. Taking aim, a primal instinct. Such an old-fashioned idea.

He hadn't been on the hunt for Nina. With her it had all just happened. He'd liked that. Nina thought his eyes were so beautiful, so blue, so full of expectation. She'd caught them in her laser gaze, from when he first shook her hand, until they kissed. That's what you called a weapon: more advanced, more subtle, and maybe more dangerous than his, the man's. All right, Tycho thought. Me, the man.

He went to one of the sinks and looked at himself. The door opened. Tycho quickly nudged up the faucet handle and started washing his hands. He glanced up at the reflection in the mirror. The boy who walked in was about his age and height. Dark hair, almost black, dark eyebrows too, and friendly eyes. He was wearing a bright blue T-shirt and skinny jeans. Tycho turned off the tap, turned around, and waved his hands under the towel dispenser. The boy turned too and said, "Hi. You must be Tycho."

T HINNING PLUMS IS SOMETHING you do in the summer, when they're still small and hard and green and hang in bunches. You lug a ladder into the orchard, lean it against the first tree, and climb up. You close your fingers around a bunch and tug: four, five plums come loose and fall down, thudding onto the ground. You climb up a little higher. You grab one handful after another. You grip onto a branch with your legs so you can get at the farthest bunches.

Nina is there too. You don't know her. Your boss says, "I trust that between the two of you, you can manage all of these plums." He winks at you. Nina climbs into one tree, you take the other. You don't see her, all you can see is leaves, but the branches of your trees are intertwined. You talk and talk. The sun is shining and there's a warm breeze blowing.

You stay late, because it pays more. Darkness falls and you keep talking. About all sorts of things. About school. About summer vacation. About friendship. About sex. You're really open. It's as if one word pulls out the next. As if you're seduced by your own words.

The crotch of your jeans rubs against the tree trunk. Twigs against your skin. Hay fever in your stomach.

And then Nina says: "Wanna come to my place? My parents are out."

H E'D WANTED TO KNOW what it was like for a long time. Sometimes it had seemed like it was all his classmates wanted to talk about, but for some reason he preferred to change the subject rather than listen to them. For a while he told himself that sex was like driving lessons—something for the future, for when he was older. Later on it just felt inconceivable. He simply couldn't picture himself walking up to a girl and starting a conversation, his eyes twinkling.

But Nina had come along and taken him by the hand. As he'd cycled home that night from her place, there was a strange sort of pride in the way he pushed on the pedals. He felt like a wise old man and a young knight at the same time. I'm in on it now, he thought. I know what they're talking about.

When he got home, there was a note from his mother on his pillow: *You're home late, but that's okay. Sweet dreams.*

He threw his clothes over the desk chair, turned down the covers, and heard his phone vibrate in his pants. It was Nina. He picked up.

"How was the ride home?"

"Yeah, fine."

"I just wanted to hear your voice for a moment."

"Oh."

"And I wanted to say I thought it was really special tonight."

"Me too."

"How do you feel?"

"Good. Kinda tired."

"Me too. I'm lying here thinking of you."

"Yeah? That's sweet."

"Are you lying in bed too?"

"Yeah."

"Okay."

Tycho tried to stifle a yawn, but failed. "I think I'm gonna go to sleep. Sleep well, okay? And, um . . . thank you."

"Oh, okay, Tycho. Yeah, me too. Good night, then."

HIS PARENTS WERE GOING to the campsite in Southampton for the nineteenth summer running. "No," he told them, "I'm not coming." He wanted to go to America. He'd looked around online, found the home page of an international kids' camp, and sent them an email. A few weeks later a letter from Knoxville, Tennessee, arrived in the mail telling him he'd been selected. "Dear Tycho, welcome to our Little World Organization. It's going to be great!"

OLIVER KJELSBERG FROM GJØVIK, Norway, had gotten the letter too. He'd remembered Tycho's name and recognized him from the camp logo on his shirt. Now they were sitting side by side in the middle of Amsterdam Airport and Oliver was speaking English with a funny accent. His sentences were short and clear, with a lilting tone, and when he started talking about football he used gestures to complement his words, his fingers drawing curves and circles in the air. To anyone walking past it might have looked like he was writing math on an imaginary blackboard, but Oliver was trying to explain to Tycho that football was a form of abstract art.

"It's all about the lines, you know? Look—here's Frank de Boer."

He slammed his fist down on the table.

Bam. There he was. Frank de Boer.

"Here are the others."

Bam, bam, bam, half a football team.

"And then here you have like a clear line."

His index finger traced a curve between three or four opposing players.

"Like a tunnel, you see? And right now de Boer doesn't see anyone at the other end, but he knows in one or two seconds Jari Litmanen is *going* to be there. And Litmanen sprints to the end of the imaginary tunnel and gets there just in time to receive the ball. See?"

Tycho did see, but there were still some other players on the table.

"That's Laudrup—do you know who that is? He runs forward, tapping the ball ahead of him three, four times as he goes. Then he passes, and look, the striker is waiting. Or this one. Or him." Tycho looked at Oliver. His eyes were shining. He held up his hands, like he was holding up a trophy. "I still can't believe I'm here. In Amsterdam! Home of Ajax! I love Barcelona, but I love Ajax too."

"I know almost nothing about football," Tycho said. "But if you come and visit me after the camp, I'll show you around the city . . . and the stadium."

"Deal!" Oliver said, holding out his hand. Tycho touched his fingers against Oliver's and looked at him. Oliver's pupils didn't flinch—they widened.

IN THE WEEKS BEFORE he left, he'd had the strange, inescapable feeling that he'd been occupied. Like a village in wartime. Nina had added herself to him—it was like riding a tandem bicycle, as if someone else was constantly pedaling along behind him.

In the days after that first late-night phone call, she flooded him with texts. If he didn't reply quickly enough, she'd write: *Call me.* Or she'd call him. At dinner, at his grandma's, even once when he was on the toilet. She'd start talking right off the bat. Telling him how in love she was. How proud she was that he loved her. That she thought he was handsome. That she thought she was pretty. That she couldn't stop thinking about him. That she'd told her family. That the dumbest love songs were all fantastic, were all so true. That she wanted to see him a lot more often. Could she come over?

More and more Tycho felt like slamming on the brakes, but Nina was relentless. Tycho didn't know how he felt about it. He felt all kinds of things at once: pride and excitement and bewilderment, irritation and interest, pity, anger and surprise and panic, all spinning around in his head like a wheel of fortune. When he made his decision and it finally slowed to a halt, all he felt was a great sense of calm—calm and resolve.

He invited her over. Another night, another bedroom—his, this time. And the moment she sat down, he ended it. He had been dreading it, but the words just popped into his mouth.

She cried. He grabbed some tissues. She left.

As she got on her bike, she said, "You asshole! Couldn't you have just done that over the phone?"

Tycho didn't know how to respond. He understood that she was angry, and he also felt like something had failed, something that could have turned out much better, but at the same time he was so hugely relieved.

"Who was that?" his mother asked. "Did you have someone over?"

"No one," he said, "no one!" and he ran up the stairs to his room, three or four at a time.

THEY WALKED DOWN THE tunnel and were greeted by a group of flight attendants. While Tycho strode past their smiling faces and onto the plane, he heard Oliver's voice behind him: "Hello! Is the airplane full? Do you think I can sit with my friend?"

One of the flight attendants said, "We'll see what we can do," and smiled. Oliver smiled back and before they knew it a woman had offered to move for them. They shoved their bags into the overhead compartments and sat down. Next to each other.

"That okay with you?" Oliver grinned.

Tycho thought he meant them sitting together, but Oliver stuck out his hand again: "Friends?"

Tycho grabbed it and said, "Of course." He felt something pink creeping across his cheeks, because he'd taken it a little too quickly, but Oliver was still beaming at him. Like a team captain who puts an arm around his opponent's shoulder before the game.

A YEAR OFF," TYCHO said. "Maybe I'll get a job for a while. And then college. To study Dutch, maybe."

"Physical therapy," Oliver said, "if I get a place in school. I'm too old to play football professionally. I should already have been scouted by now."

"How bad did you want that?"

"Dunno. Real bad, sometimes. But I gave up on a big tournament to go to Little World. I didn't feel like being cooped up at home for three weeks first, with Mom on safari and Dad baking in the Spanish sun."

The flight attendants fanned out into the aisles and started gesturing toward the emergency exits, more or less in sync, followed by another routine with life vests.

"Look," Tycho said to Oliver. "Ballet."

"Shh," said Oliver. "We're moving."

The plane slowly taxied to the runway.

I N TYCHO'S TOP 10 of people that were easiest to talk to, women in their thirties and forties ranked first. Small children came in second, then girls and old people, and further, much further down, boys.

Last, by quite a long way, were grown men. It had been that way ever since he was a kid. When he went to a classmate's house for a playdate, he'd ask the mothers about their work and usually he'd get candy and compliments. The fathers he would try to avoid.

Of course later it had become easier. In high school he'd started spending his lunch breaks hanging out in the bicycle shed with the other boys. Even so, he was one of the few who also hung out on the steps in front of the school. That's where the two groups would mix, though the girls were in the vast majority. They'd talk about what he was wearing, what he'd done with his hair. In return he'd put an arm around them from time to time, their long hair tickling his skin.

But this Norwegian boy, this Oliver, seemed to defy every category. And if forging a friendship took time and space, six or seven miles of altitude and six or seven hours were plenty for Oliver and Tycho. By the time they changed planes in Atlanta, they dashed side by side into the Plane Train as if they'd been traveling together all their lives.

THE LITTLE WORLD ORGANIZATION had started in the dreams of a sweet old lady. She'd dreamt about children from all over the world, beaming with happiness, with nothing but play on their minds. Children who, once they were all grown up and were ministers, ambassadors, and sergeant majors, would put down their work every once in a while to think about all their old friends from overseas. And about peace.

One day that inspired old lady founded the Little World Organization. At first it had just been a small group of dreamers, but nowadays there were branches in a whole bunch of different countries. Every summer there were between forty and fifty Little World camps all over the world. Ten international delegations came to each camp: two boys and two girls, all ten years old, accompanied by an adult leader.

Then there was a staff team—three people from the host country, assisted by four junior assistants around eighteen years old: Tycho, Oliver, and two American girls they'd soon be meeting.

They were coming together for a month of vacation in a miniature world, where everything was fine, everyone was okay, and they found friendships that crossed borders.

T HEY HEARD SINGING AND laughter. And when the doors whooshed open—the doors to the arrivals hall, the doors to their Little World—they saw a huge group of people arranged like a royal family on a balcony. Everyone waved at them.

But when Oliver and Tycho took another three or four steps toward them, the welcoming committee broke apart. Someone took their suitcases from them, arms were slung around their shoulders, and before they knew it they were being presented to the three people who formed the core of the group. Three dark purple polo shirts with white letters saying *Knoxville's Little World—The Staff*. A short woman in her mid-forties ("Hi! My name is Carol!"), a tall, thin guy with a beard ("Hey, I'm Gary"), and the head honcho, the biggest and strongest of the three, who gave each of them, in turn, a fervent hug. "Welcome," he said, "welcome to America. I'm your camp director. Call me John." He smiled, the way men smile when they feel responsible for something—proud and determined and a little sad. His hair was thin. He was wearing a button that read, *They Tell Me I'm the Boss*.

"You guys hungry?" Gary said. They nodded and were led to a Burger King, where other recent arrivals were sitting at a long table—delegation leaders from various countries: Denmark, Ireland, Uruguay, all in their twenties and thirties. The kids they'd brought with them had already been picked up by host families. For the first day or so it would just be adults at the camp so they could prepare and get to know each other. Tycho sat down at the table and Oliver squeezed in beside him—even though there was more room next to the others.

T HEY WERE CRAMMED HAPHAZARDLY into an air-conditioned van, much like their suitcases, which had been stuffed into another vehicle.

There wasn't enough room. Oliver was half-sitting on the lap of the Mexican delegation leader, and an arm from Josine, the leader from Martinique, was draped over Tycho's shoulder.

Gary drove and kept the conversation going. Everyone was tired, but they still tried to respond to things he was saying about Knoxville, about the city hall, the baseball team, the hefty fines you got if you threw candy wrappers out the window onto the highway. Before long they were tentatively comparing notes about the different rules in their various countries, while the air-conditioning mixed their breaths into one. Once they arrived, they found they had to mix again, this time with the group that had arrived earlier that day and had already explored the location of the camp: a public high school, empty for summer vacation.

I N T H E V A N, M O S T attention had eventually focused on Yoshiyuki, the leader from Japan.

"Yoshi. Call me Yoshi," he said, so they did just that. He was the one who, even though he seemed shy and perfectly polite at first, made things so much easier by starting conversations with each and every one.

Days later, when Oliver and Tycho were recapping those first moments before bed, discussing who they'd seen doing what, they would conclude that Yoshi had been the one that, just by being friendly, had linked them all together—he kept practicing their names out loud, asking people where they were from, and what they liked, silently giving everyone the chance to go over the names and faces.

B Y THE TIME EVERYONE had arrived, and all of them were drinking Coke in the cafeteria—the ten leaders, the junior assistants, and the camp staff— Yoshi had already single-handedly broken the ice of their Little World.

John, the camp director, got up. He waited a moment for everyone to settle down. Then, he grinned and said, "Friends!"

He gave a speech about "teamwork," about "trust" and "love." He explained why this camp was going to be special for all of them and said that he, Carol, and Gary already knew they would never forget these weeks. Everyone was quiet. Most were staring at the glasses on the plastic tablecloth, or at their fingertips. Or at someone else's fingertips. But as the director spoke more about "spirit" and "fun," heads began to pop up. He knew how to use words to kindle a flame. And he knew that a fire needed to be fed, because he ended his speech by announcing a pool party that same night, at the home of the Knoxville Little World CEO.

Someone shouted, "Yeah!" and a few others even started applauding.

"One more thing," John said. "You're all gonna have to turn in your cellphones. But you guys already knew that, right? You can get them back in your free period every other day. Here at Little World, we're all about real, face-to-face contact." He grinned.

Yes, they already knew that. There was an emergency number for parents who urgently needed to get in touch, but that was more for the kids than for the four "juniors." Tycho had promised his mother and father that he'd message them every now and then, but they knew he wouldn't be spending all day glued to his phone or a computer. They didn't do that either. And besides, their campsite had poor reception.

"Let's go!" John said—and everyone grabbed their suitcase and went off in search of a bed.

OLIVER AND TYCHO WOULD be sharing a supply closet.

There were no more rooms. The twenty ten-year-old boys who were arriving in two days' time would be sleeping in the art classroom. At the back of that room there was a door that led to a storage space crammed with pottery wheels, stools, screws, pliers, and even a loom—all carefully locked away behind see-through chest doors. Now a bunk bed had been squeezed in there too. Oliver claimed the top. His mattress would be the sky Tycho gazed up at.

TYCHO DIVVIED UP THE tiny wardrobe. Oliver was trying to pull the wrinkles out of a button-down shirt. "What do you think of them?" he asked.

"Who?" Tycho said.

"The girls." The American girls, Sherilynn and Donna, their fellow junior assistants.

"Oh, yeah. They seem like fun. Donna is sweet. She seems like the kind of person you can talk to."

"I'm sure we'll have a great time, the four of us."

"Yeah," Tycho said. "Yeah."

THE FEMALE LEADERS WERE sitting together, except for Josine, the leader from Martinique, who was swimming laps in the pool with Carol. The male leaders were standing around the barbecue. The taco bar had been cleaned out. The camp director and Gary were drinking whiskey with the CEO from glasses piled high with ice cubes.

Oliver and Tycho were sitting on the diving board, with Sherilynn—long, brown hair and eyelashes other people only have in beauty commercials—and Donna—tall and alive, with a face that was an open invitation to confide your secrets to—floating in the water around them. But if you glanced their way every few minutes, you'd soon lose count of how often that configuration kept changing—next time you looked up, it would be Oliver and Tycho in the water, and eventually everyone ended up in there. The CEO had someone get bathrobes for them, which they would shrug on only to take them off again moments later.

"Looks like our junior assistants are getting along just fine." John, the camp director, chuckled, and the CEO's wife thought it was all "very sweet."

IT GOT LATE. THEY'D lit tiki torches and the pool had underwater lighting. Here and there people were chatting. Somewhere in the house, Gary was strumming a guitar. Snatches of songs came drifting through the window.

It was a warm night and Tycho was falling asleep now and then, fighting his jet lag. Oliver had discovered some deck chairs. They started tussling over who was getting one—there were only three—but then Sherilynn put one of them away and squeezed in next to Oliver between the armrests of deck chair number two. Donna grabbed Tycho's hand and pulled him down into the other one. No one was paying them any attention, although every now and then the hostess would bring them another carafe of lemonade.

Later, Tycho couldn't quite remember what was real and what he had dreamed. Snippets of footage tugged at his mind: whispering in his ear, Donna's soft hair, someone calling: 'I found wine! I found wine!' All of them drinking secretly, Oliver and Sherilynn kissing, a garden shed, an empty bottle clinking on some stones, Carol shining a flashlight and saying that it was late. Feet stepping into a car. Lights along the side of the road. Their supply closet. His fingers knitted together to help Oliver up onto the top bunk. Suppressed giggling. The pillow, so wonderfully cool. Then nothing.

WHEN TYCHO WOKE UP, he saw Oliver, puking into a plastic bag. His strong legs poked out from under his boxer shorts, white and shaky. After throwing up three times he turned around and said, "Sorry."

"That's okay," said Tycho. "Must have been the wine."

"Yeah," Oliver said. "The wine. The whole night, really."

"Can't believe we did all that," Tycho said. "You?"

"I hardly ever drink," Oliver said. "I'm trying to be a responsible athlete, usually."

He started laughing, but choked. A strand of spittle shot out onto his chin. Tycho threw him a towel.

Then there was a knock on the door, and they heard Gary's voice, much too awake: "Breakfast!" Oliver and Tycho groaned in unison, then burst out laughing at the stereo effect.

THE HALLWAYS OF THE school smelled clean and abandoned—but behind that smell there still was a whiff of sweat, the echo of giggling, worrying, indifferent students. The walls were lined with portraits of alumni. On their way to the cafeteria, Tycho thought for a moment that Nina was staring out at him from one of the frames. Nina, he thought, here? But then he walked into the cafeteria and looked around for Donna. She didn't come over to join him. She was whispering with Sherilynn. Tycho surveyed the room. Oliver was sitting with the camp director.

He ended up talking to Brahim from Egypt. There was a little stadium in front of the school: a rubber track and a small set of bleachers, eight or nine rows. Brahim had already been there. He'd gone jogging. He asked why Tycho wasn't eating, but before Tycho could answer, they heard Carol's voice over the PA system: "Time for the flag ceremony. Everyone to the flagpole."

Right, the flagpole. Tycho had forgotten the words to the song. He hadn't practiced much back in the Netherlands. He did remember how they were all supposed to stand: in a large circle around the flagpole, with their arms crossed right over left, hand in hand with the person on either side of them. Feet firmly planted on the ground and head held high, eyes on the pole as the flag was being hoisted. And all together now—

Learn a lesson, make a friend
In these valleys, in this land
Here we stand and think and talk
Take a journey, take a walk.

Little world for me and you
Let this world be bright and new
All of us can feel at ease
spread the joy and
spread the peace!

Tycho looked around the circle—gingerly, not too fast, because even just moving his eyes hurt. Here I am, he thought, and I'm already beginning to forget what my room back home looks like. Already I'm confusing Nina's face with that of a total stranger. That's how easy it is: trading one world for the other. As long as you keep walking, flying, running around like everyone else.

Donna, who had ended up next to him after all— just like that, almost by accident—squeezed his hand. Why? Because of what they were singing? ". . . *for me and you*"? What exactly had happened the previous night? Tycho racked his brain, but the hammering in his brain drowned out everything he turned up.

THEY GOT TO USE their phones, if they brought one, and Tycho texted his mother: *All good here. Carol is the staff member in charge of us juniors. She's really nice. The other assistant, Oliver, from Norway, is awesome. They keep using that word here: awesome. The girls are nice too. Hope you're having fun in Southampton. Bye from the States.*

Her reply: *Great. Have fun.*

His mother had probably wanted to write more, but Tycho knew she didn't like typing on her phone. And the reception out in the countryside wasn't great.

X, he wrote.

X, she wrote.

CAROL PUT TYCHO, DONNA, Sherilynn, and Oliver to work. One chore knocked into the next like a row of dominoes. The hours fell away and slowly all the items on Carol's list were checked off. Tycho's headache gradually disappeared, and a strange cheerfulness came over him. Last night was over. No more winks, no more fooling around by the pool. He taught Donna how to say good morning in Dutch—"goeiemorgen," with that typical guttural "g"—and he and Oliver played a game of who-knows-their-national-anthem-by-heart.

THEY WERE SITTING EATING popsicles when some of the leaders started jumping up to look out the window, sitting down, then jumping up again, their chatter getting a little louder each time, like the rising line on a fever chart: *the kids are coming!* It was like forty different heads of state would be getting out of the host families' cars in ten minutes' time. The excitement was infectious—the juniors rose to their feet too. Oliver ran back and forth to the track, just to move around, and Sherilynn and Donna were giggling.

There was something Tycho still had to do. Something he had to ask. Something he wanted to know for sure. He asked Donna to walk with him for a moment.

"Why?" she said.

"Just come with me a sec," he said. Outside, in the bright sun, he asked: "What happened between us last night?"

"Nothing happened," she said, "nothing that would get in the way of us being friends. Just friends. I have a boyfriend, you see."

Tycho stopped and grinned. How silly to be standing there, grinning, he thought. But he was.

She pushed up her sunglasses and looked at him. Pretty gray eyes. Soft hair. Freckles. Dimples in her cheeks. He gave her an amiable smile. Moments later, he thought: No, of course nothing happened. I knew it. I just wanted to know that she knew too. As they were walking back, he tapped two fingers against her cheek. Donna made as if to ruffle his hair.

CAR DOORS SLAMMED SHUT: host fathers and mothers for a day. Host parents to children they could barely understand half the time. Still, they were all saying goodbye with hugs and kisses. The leaders were happy, the kids impressed. In the midst of all the hubbub, Tycho, Sherilynn, Oliver, and Donna were running around lugging bags and shaking hands. Carol and Director John were talking to the host families— thank you so much, see you soon, is there room at the inn for weekend number two?

Tycho helped a few of the boys unpack. Most of them had already disappeared: thrown their bags onto a bed, run three circles around the dorm, and then headed off to the stadium with Oliver and Brahim for their first international football game.

SIX THIRTY: DINNERTIME AT the camp. There was so much to see, so much to hear. Tycho's attention zoomed in and out. He was standing behind the kitchen counter with Oliver, dishing out mashed potatoes. He looked from one child to the next, at what his own hands were doing, at what else was going on in the cafeteria. The line of children was splitting up into small groups that claimed tables by slamming down trays and pulling back chairs, the legs screeching against the floor. There were words in all sorts of languages. Utensils glinting in the light. So many voices, so many colors.

But from up close they were just faces. Hands. Necks. T-shirts. The Swedish kids that Tycho had ended up sitting with were hyped up. They were fidgeting in their seats, wolfing down their food, and shouting—all at the same time. Tycho was flipping between talking to their leader and talking to them, trying to keep them from launching their string beans at each other.

He looked around for Donna. She was braiding an Uruguayan girl's ponytail. Oliver was sitting with the Irish delegation. Both of the boys were called Paddy, Paddy One and Paddy Two, and Oliver seemed to be talking about the offside rule: Tycho saw his friend's fingers passing the ball in the air.

"Oh no you don't!" Tycho was just in time to intercept a spoon, on its way across the table toward someone else's mashed potatoes.

E VENING CAME AND WITH it a new set of snapshots. Kids' legs, pulled up into triangles, sprawled out on the floor, tucked under backsides, or stretched out so that you almost tripped over them. All the boys and girls were sitting on the tiled floor of the common room, leaning against each other and their leaders.

Director John launched into a new speech, pausing now and then so the leaders could translate. Friendship, love, and understanding—they all seemed to use the same sort of sign language to get those concepts across. Next Carol leapt up. She did some kind of trick with a bag of confetti—Tycho wasn't paying attention, because Sherilynn was tracing letters onto Oliver's back, and Tycho wanted to know which ones. And why.

Time for the song and the flag again: arms crossed, yes, like that, right over left, and then good night, sleep tight. Lights out in the dorms just past ten. Chatter and squeals of laughter coming through the doors. Two delegation leaders were on duty outside the girls' dorm, two more were posted in front of the boys'. The others were chilling out in the leaders' room, drinking Coke and Mountain Dew and Dr Pepper, with Tycho and Donna operating the vending machine. Oliver and Sherilynn were outside somewhere. Where, Tycho wondered, where?

It got late and everyone saw the Swedish leader start to make out with Virginía, the leader from Uruguay. Tycho heard Carol say that sparks always fly at Little World. He headed to bed. He wanted to talk through everything that had happened that day. With Oliver. But he guessed Oliver was out lying in the moonlight somewhere.

The sound of Tycho's feet trudging down the corridor: never mind, never mind.

ALL THE BOYS WERE asleep. Little sighing mounds throughout the classroom. Tycho tiptoed over to the supply closet. He didn't turn the big lights on.

"Hey!" Oliver said. He was right there, lying in the top bunk. His eyes open.

"Hey," Tycho said. "You're still up?"

"I couldn't get to sleep."

"Too much . . . going on?"

"How do you mean?"

"Outside?"

"Oh. Yeah. Something like that."

Tycho wasn't sure if he wanted to know. He took off his T-shirt. It was a strange feeling knowing that someone was watching.

"I didn't sleep with her, if that's what you mean."

Tycho nodded and sat down.

"Okay," he said, "okay." And waited.

Oliver jumped off the top bunk and sat down next to Tycho—legs wide, his elbows planted on his knees, his hands already gesturing, as if the air had to be stirred for his words to rise to the surface.

"You know, she wanted to. She really did."

"What about you?"

"I didn't. I mean—I like her. But not like that."

"And did you tell her that?"

"I didn't get the chance. We went outside for a minute and we were talking and then all of a sudden she wanted me to hug her."

"Whoa. And then what?"

"Then I walked away."

Tycho's face grew hot. Not with shame, he was sure of that. But he didn't get a chance to figure out the real reason, because of the roaring inside his head, like the roar that football players let out when they've scored a goal. And just like the players, who have to run back to their positions when the cheering dies down so the game can start again, Tycho came straight back down to Earth. He was sitting next to Oliver and Oliver had a problem and had come to him, his friend, for advice.

"But yesterday, when we were by the pool, you kissed her, didn't you?"

"Yea. Sort of. She kissed me. And I'd had that wine, remember?"

"Right. And then I had to help you into bed."

They both laughed. "I have, like, no alcohol tolerance."

"Want an aspirin?"

"Where did you get those?"

"My bag. My mom packed them."

"Aww. Did Mommy—"

"Don't you bring my mother into this! I'd rather have a mom who cares about me than a splitting headache."

They laughed, and Oliver climbed back up onto his bunk. Tycho took off his jeans, crawled into his sleeping bag, and turned off the little light. His cheeks had cooled down a little, as if all this talk about aspirin had helped. He whispered "god natt" and Oliver wished him "welterusten"—they'd taught each other that a long, long time ago, somewhere over England. Then he rolled over, turning his back on everything that had happened that day.

B UT NO—HE DIDN'T fall asleep yet. Thoughts sprang back up like the grass on a football pitch an hour after the game. He realized that he *hadn't* helped his friend. He'd just listened—he hadn't said anything. He hadn't told him about Donna. Or about himself. Or how glad he was that he didn't have to share Oliver with anyone. Glad that Oliver was available. He realized that it might affect the whole camp if Sherilynn and Oliver couldn't work together any-more. Maybe he should discuss it with Donna. But then again, maybe not. At the end of the day, he didn't really care about the camp.

Then he ended up drifting off after all. Until he was jolted awake, because an idea occurred to him. Days are like migrating birds: they all fly in the same direc-tion, he thought. But some stubbornly follow their own course, and end up determining the route for the rest.

This day fell into that category.

T HE NEXT MORNING THEY went swimming. Everyone piled into a minivan and they were taken to the local pool. Before long the fastest kids were jumping off the low diving board, while the brav-est leapt off the high one. Tycho was among them. He loved water, although the way things worked here took some getting used to.

They had to put on numbered plastic caps and there was a raised chair at the edge of the pool. Perched up there was a lifeguard who kept an eye on people. At the slightest misbehavior he'd yell a penalty: "OUT—for three minutes, OUT—five minutes!"

T HEY'D BEEN SWIMMING FOR an hour when, suddenly, without Tycho wanting them to, all sorts of things started happening.

OLIVER WALKED AWAY. To get dressed, he said. Why? Had he had enough of swimming? Tycho wanted to ask where he was going, to tell him "wait, stay"—but the girls from Japan were dragging him up the steps to the slide. After he'd whooshed down, he left the pool area. Just to see where Oliver had gone off to. To maybe talk to him for a minute. Or just to use the restroom, at least.

The exit from the pool branched into the different shower areas, boys and girls. You had to pass through yours to get to the changing rooms.

And that's where Tycho saw what he saw.

OLIVER WAS STANDING IN the middle of the men's shower area, alone. The sun was coming in through the upper windows. A beam of light fell diagonally onto a thousand white tiles. And in the middle of that light, between rows of spraying showerheads—nine to the left, nine to the right—water was streaming down Oliver's face. His eyes were closed. His hair clung to his head. His chest, his abdomen, his legs were a river. He had taken off his swimming trunks, they were dangling from one finger, and he was standing there—naked, simple, proud, without shame, entirely content—enjoying the hot water.

As if something or someone had suddenly cupped Tycho's head between two warm hands—that's what it felt like. As if a can of silver paint was pouring all over his body.

Shit, Tycho thought. Shit.

T HERE WAS NOTHING HE could say. Nothing he could do. Except back away, one foot, one heel at a time, until after about ten feet he turned around, took a running start, and made the biggest splash the little pool had seen in a long time.

Immediately boys were jumping up onto his shoulders. He grabbed them by the waist and flung them this way and that. They shrieked. Everyone was swept up in it, excited and laughing. Wild. He threw children around and roared. He got himself barred from the pool for being too rowdy, and so he ran through the now empty shower room to the one place where he could be alone for a moment—a toilet stall.

There he stood, panting, his hands gripping the top of the stall door. Time passed. A minute? Two, three, four? His breath grew even again. But then suddenly his body was in a hot rush to pull off his swimming trunks—quick, quick, lift up your feet and throw them into a corner—and there he stood, his fingers curled around, and released all of his pent-up excitement.

A FTERWARDS HE HEADED TO one of the changing cubicles, trembling. That's where he was sitting now, staring down at the floor, a large, soft towel slung around his shoulders. He smelled the fabric softener his mother had used—the comfort of home reaching all the way to Knoxville.

A storm was surging inside his head. Old thoughts, dreams, fantasies, things he'd read, things he'd felt, all swirling in a vortex. He thought of his father. His mother. His father again. His friends. One friend in the seventh grade. A teacher. Two or three celebrities. A TV host. The singer in a boy band. An uncle. Nina. Donna. But underneath, between, on top of everything else, he thought of Oliver. How he'd stood there, like a waterfall, a rock. He remembered how they'd met, like he was seeing it in the rearview mirror. He'd probably felt it even then. And from deep inside, a broad smile spread across his face.

Men, he thought. Hunters. Ha.

FOR A LONG TIME, there'd been something he'd chosen not to see. Just like you might sit on a beach and notice the people around you, all pointing up at the sky. You know they're seeing an airplane, an airplane with a banner, a banner with a message anyone can read—but no, you don't look, because you don't feel like it.

There'd always been something, and he hadn't looked. But now Tycho was looking. Now he saw everything. The whole wide sky.

HE KNEW HE HAD to call it being in love. Crazy in love. Head-over-heels in love. But that all sounded too meager, too accidental. He racked his brain for something else to call it. Transformation? Foolishness? He felt transformed, and he felt like a fool.

No matter what he called it, it had flooded him. It had made him light. And heavy. He felt higher, deeper, more real.

DONNA CAME AND SAT down next to him. She slapped his thigh and said, "You're not really in love with me, are you?"

Tycho looked up at her.

She laughed. "But you are in love with someone else?"

Tycho looked away. Being in love, he realized, messes with your navigation. You have a hard time steering the ship, butterflies keep clouding your field of vision, but despite all that, Tycho had decided one thing: he didn't want Oliver to know. He was keeping this to himself.

But then she asked again. And again. And the next day—they were standing in the kitchen stirring a pot, no one else around—and so he told Donna after all. As he talked, he heard himself say the things that he'd spent an evening and a night, a morning and an afternoon thinking. And it felt true and new.

He wasn't worried about what she thought. He didn't even look at her as he was talking—well, he looked, but he didn't see her, he only saw himself. It wasn't until later, when he'd tripped over his story and told it another three or four times, that he noticed she was beaming. As if his good mood had rubbed off on her.

But Oliver wasn't allowed to know.

"You're crazy," Donna said, "why don't you just tell him?"

"No!" Tycho said. He imagined how startled Oliver

would be, and how he'd say, "Tych, I like you, but not like that." That's what he'd told Nina, and he'd crushed her with those words. Nothing could be worse than that.

"I have a brother," Donna said, "who's just like you."

"Come on," Tycho said, "let's go, we have to go play Human Origami."

TYCHO PLAYED AT BEING junior assistant in a camp that suspected nothing. Where everything rolled along like it was supposed to. Sometimes, he avoided Oliver. Not too often, but when he was with him Tycho felt like a house split into two floors. His first floor was safe and familiar. From down there he talked and laughed and went through the motions of their established friendship. As if he hadn't noticed that another floor had been built on top, didn't know what was going on just a little further upstairs. He firmly locked the elevator to that top floor when he and Oliver walked into their supply closet at night, though he was aware that someone inside him was looking down from up there, someone who'd started looking at Oliver's back, at his chest, his biceps, the edges of his boxer shorts, and he could hear that person's heart pounding. Loudly, so loudly that downstairs you no longer knew what time it was, or what was being said, and you missed the doorbell ringing.

But eventually it would get too late to keep talking, and he'd be staring up at the safe mattress sky above him.

T HERE WERE NATIONAL EVENINGS. One delegation after another would spend an evening pretending the camp had relocated to their own country. To Ireland. Denmark. Then Mexico. There were enchiladas and an embroidered napkin for everyone, followed by a dance. The Mexican boys wore sombreros and the girls wore dresses with lace and ruffled sleeves and big swishy skirts.

It took his mind off things. Tycho watched and Tycho laughed, Tycho danced and played games. He always knew where and how many feet away from him Oliver was, but he wanted people to think of him as the junior assistant who was enjoying every Little World minute. Which he was—just not in the way they thought.

C AROL DRAGGED OVER A cushion. "Hey, how's it going?"

Tycho drew back, smiled, and said "Good."

"Are you having a nice time in our Little World?"

"Yeah, of course!"

"I'm glad," Carol said, folding up her legs to form a cushion on top of a cushion. "My son is the same age as you. He's at a Little World camp in Canada right now. I talked to him on the phone. They were having issues. He's not getting along with the other assistants. I told him that things are going really well with you guys. Right?"

She looked over at him. He nodded.

"Between Oliver and Sherilynn too?"

"I don't know," Tycho said, a little too quickly and a little too loudly. He hurriedly asked, "Do you miss him? Your son, I mean."

"Not yet. But when it hits me, I'll just project my motherly feelings onto you. I'll just think of you guys as my temporary children, if you don't mind?" She smiled.

"Not at all," Tycho said.

"Thanks," Carol said. As she got up, her face appeared in his sight line. She pinched his cheek between her thumb and forefinger and said, "You big boy, you!"

She laughed.

G ARY ASKED IF TYCHO could sing "Brother Jacob" in Dutch. He was collecting all the different versions of that song. He grabbed his guitar and sang it in Swedish and Norwegian and Finnish and German and French. How did the Dutch one go?

Tycho felt dorky singing this old-fashioned song, but he still did it. He didn't want anyone to notice anything. He glanced over at Oliver, who was sitting on a bench, his arm draped behind Sherilynn. Around her shoulders? On the back of the seat? Tycho shifted over a bit so he could see better—on the back of the seat, thankfully. But what was the deal?

"Bim, bam, bom," Gary sang. "Bim, bam, bom."

FOUR WEEKS, THAT'S KIND of a long time," Oliver said. "I'm already getting sick of these games."

Talking about the camp and about the others—thank God there was that, once they were back in their room at night. "Do you want to go home?" Tycho asked.

"No, not really. But I kind of wish we could be replaced halfway through. We could go to Amsterdam. Or somewhere else."

"We?" Tycho said. He poked his head out from the lower bunk. The sudden groundswell inside of him almost caused him to choke. Oliver was lying above him, talking to the ceiling, his arms folded behind his head.

"Yeah." He rolled over onto his side and looked down at Tycho. "Anyway, what do you see in Donna?"

"I dunno," Tycho said. He could feel his cheeks burning. "Just someone to talk to sometimes."

"That's all?"

"Yeah, of course!" Tycho fixed his bright eyes on Oliver, his gaze like the exclamation marks after his words.

"Okay, okay." Oliver laughed. "I talked to Sherilynn, by the way. That day we took the kids to the pool. She wasn't swimming because she was on her period, and suddenly I thought: I'm gonna go over and talk to her. And so I told her what the deal was. That was good, right?" He turned over onto his back again.

"Very good," Tycho said.

But then he stopped talking, because he was afraid his pounding heart would come leaping out of his mouth.

I T WAS AFTER MIDNIGHT and Tycho said, "It's getting harder." Donna was asking him how he managed to fake it every day. "It's getting harder." He wanted to say the days were like a funnel. In the mornings and the afternoon things were easy, when he and Oliver were immersed in the bustle of the camp, playing games, organizing group activities. The kids diluted his focus on Oliver, though he always knew where Oliver was and what he was doing, as if a sonar system had been installed in his brain. But at night, once the kids had been put to bed, and the chatter had died down, it became more difficult. That was when he got Oliver, pure and concentrated.

At night the junior assistants had kitchen duty. They had to set the tables for breakfast and put out place cards to change up the seating, because everyone had to mingle at mealtimes—the point of Little World was contact, contact, contact. Once they were done, they'd pull up stools around the fridge and grab a soda—they didn't have to pay for it here. Sometimes Carol would stop by, or Josine, or Brahim. They'd play music, and chat, and the funnel would get narrower and narrower.

And then, later still, in the small hours, the neck of the funnel ended in their supply closet, where Tycho had to pretend that in his eyes, too, they were just buddies. Best friends, closer every day, but not much more, nothing else. That was the hardest part, he'd wanted to tell Donna, but it turned out she had asked her question because there was something she wanted to get off her chest. "Tycho, I told Sherilynn. I'm sorry, but I had no choice."

"What? Why?" Tycho said.

"Don't you get it? I had to tell her that sooner or later, you and Oliver are going to end up together.

Otherwise she'd keep being difficult. She's after him too, Tycho, surely you know that?"

". . . that Oliver and I are going to end up together?"

"Of course. It's only a matter of time. Get real, you dummy. Just look at him. It's obvious!"

It was late. Sherilynn was sitting over with the camp leaders. Oliver had already gone to bed. Tycho had told him he'd be there soon, but now he needed proof. He subjected Donna to a cross-examination that ended only when she could no longer stifle her yawns.

Tycho went to bed walking on air. He looked at Oliver breathing and breathing and breathing and began to think that—No, he thought, it's impossible, that kind of thing just doesn't happen. Not in the big world, and not in Little World.

S O THIS IS ME, Tycho thought the next morning, and one of the side effects of being in love is that once again I'm standing looking at myself in the mirror. It was still early and he was the first one in the communal bathroom. He thought: This is how Oliver sees me every morning. This is what he says good morning to. Good morning, eyes. Mouth and cheeks. Hair all sticking up. He thought about everything that was happening. He'd wanted to set his life in motion.

But this wasn't hunting—this was being pulled along by something.

"Like what you see?"

Director John came in and started noisily washing his sleepy face. He spat into the sink. Water splashed in all directions. This was probably how bears would do it too if they were standing in front of a mirror. Tycho grimaced in reply, which was enough for Director John, who remained the boss, here even in the bathroom, and perhaps had only intended his question as a "here I am." Tycho grabbed his toothpaste and started brushing.

I T WAS THE MORNING of the eighth day. Breakfast.

"Congratulations, everyone. We've got something to celebrate today. We've been together for one week," Director John said. His T-shirt was too short and the people sitting in the front could see a strip of tummy moving: when the camp director was talking, it looked like his belly button was lip-syncing. "Today we'll be going into the mountains and having a picnic. Bring your sunscreen and your good mood."

They needed to pack sandwiches. Tycho sliced open the rolls, Oliver buttered them, and Sherilynn put ham or cheese on them and then put the tops back on.

Donna slid them into plastic bags. They were a well-oiled machine, a junior assistant assembly line—until Oliver had to go help Carol lug some jerricans. He strode out of the kitchen. Donna watched him go, exchanged a glance with Sherilynn, then leaned over the table and said, "Tycho, it's been one week for you too . . ."

"Huh?" Tycho answered. He looked up, his knife hovering in midair.

"Tick, tock, tick, tock," Sherilynn said.

She held up a slice of cheese. There were holes in it.

"I don't get it," Tycho said. Seven bread rolls stared at him openmouthed from down on the table. Sherilynn started humming.

Oliver came back in.

"Are they teasing you?" he asked.

"Not just him," Donna said, and started laughing. Sherilynn joined in.

"Girls . . . !" Oliver said, looking over at Tycho.

If this is a competition, Tycho thought, then at least we're on the same team.

"They're all kinda scary," he said, returning Oliver's gaze.

Oliver grinned at him behind the girls' backs. Tycho was the only one who saw.

E VERYONE WAS SITTING IN the beds of pickup trucks. Oliver and Tycho had ended up next to each other. They were jostling over potholes and it was boiling hot. Thankfully they were shielded by trees most of the time. Dappled shadows caressed Oliver's face. Tycho heard Gary singing a song about "donnadonnadonnadohonna" and he heard Sheri-lynn laughing her head off in the second truck. But with him, beside him, around him, was Oliver's voice.

"They're different," Oliver said. Tycho's foot slipped—the pickup was bouncing all over the place—and accidentally ended up next to Oliver's. Their sneakers looked for support and found it.

"And inimitable," said Oliver. What was he saying? Tycho watched the words coming out of his mouth. His lips and the glinting wetness between them. White teeth.

"I almost never understand them." A thin film of sweat covered the side of Oliver's nose. Makeup for boys. Tycho stared at him and thought: What is he talking about? Girls?

"They're aliens," Oliver said, "or maybe *I'm* the alien."

"Of course not!" Tycho said loudly—too loudly—but Oliver started laughing, and when he gave him a whack on the shoulders—hard, too hard—Tycho thought: If you put a hundred touches together, what you get is a smack.

T HE JUNIOR ASSISTANTS DARTED between the picnic tables, serving food. Tycho felt like he was losing his mind. He spun left and right—sometimes because there was someone on the left or on the right who wanted a drink, but most of the time because Oliver was headed that way. He poured an extra drop into a cup Oliver had just filled. He exchanged cheese rolls Oliver had handed out for ham rolls. He ran around and he watched Oliver. When they'd doled out almost all of the food, he paused for a moment, but then he ran on to the next table, bumping into Oliver and saying sorry. "That's all right," Oliver said, and Tycho thought: Okay, I'm quitting now.

He sighed and went over to a table far, far away with a group of girls who were sitting whispering to each other. He sat down next to Josine, who he hadn't really had a chance to talk to until that point. He asked, "Are you having a good time so far?" and hoped she'd give a long and detailed answer.

T HEY'D BEEN TAKEN BACK to the camp in the pickup trucks. They jumped out—the sound of feet landing. Tycho walked over to Donna. He'd spent the entire ride back staring at the side of the road, the trees and the mountains, and finally he decided he should try to hang out with Donna more.

"What a great day!" Donna shouted.

"Yeah?"

"Everything was planned so well. John really is amazing!"

"Oh yeah?" Tycho said.

"Don't you think?"

"Hm. Maybe. He seems kind of full of himself."

"No! Get out of here! John? Everybody *loves* him!"

"Well, Oliver says . . ."

"That doesn't count. Of course you'll say what Oliver says. The way you two spend all day following each other around . . ."

Tycho was taken aback. "Really?"

"Well, not literally, of course. Although . . . during the picnic . . ." She giggled.

Tycho didn't know what to say. He looked around. The Irish boys came walking by. He was saved. "Hey," Tycho shouted, "what are you guys up to?"

"We don't know yet," they said.

"Oh yes you do," Tycho said gratefully, "we're going down to the track!"

He called out "See you later!" to Donna and broke into a run.

T HEY WERE SITTING IN the bleachers, all the way at the top. They'd raced each other. They'd done long jumps in the sandpit. Paddy One and Paddy Two had climbed halfway up the lampposts, Tycho had managed to lure them back down again, and now they were sitting side by side, panting.

"Does anyone know what time it is?" Tycho asked.

One of the boys showed him his watch.

"Oh shit!" Tycho yelled and jumped up. "It's dinnertime. Let's go!"

It was much too late, so they ran the whole way back.

Y OU HAVE A RESPONSIBILITY!" Gary said.

Gary, who so often came up with the games they played, who cracked jokes, shot straws out of milkshake cups, that same Gary was now giving Tycho a lecture. Tycho listened, but he didn't hear anything. He already knew. He'd brought the boys back way too late. Adele, the leader in charge of the Paddys, had been worried. Donna said she'd seen him outside. Oliver had gone looking for them. Brahim had gone looking for them. Dinnertime had come and gone. Carol had kept some food warm for them. When they got back to the camp, Gary had taken him aside, into the staff room. Gary said he was lucky the camp director wasn't around right then. He told him he had to make him a promise, which Tycho did. "I promise," he said, and then he was free to go.

I T WAS DARK WHEN he entered the common room after dinner. The Japanese children were giving a slide show. It was their National Evening. Tycho had to cross in front of the overhead projector. For a moment, he was all lit up. He felt people looking at him, or maybe just at what was being projected onto his body in that split second.

"And this is Junko at her school . . . and this is Junko in her street . . . and this is Atsu at his music lesson . . . this is Atsu with his father . . . this is Atsu with his mother . . . here's Daiji playing football . . . and this is me," Yoshi explained.

Tycho was glad that everything kept going. That they were all given little booklets in Japanese and an origami bird. That they gathered around the flag to squeeze in the Little World song before bedtime. That Paddy One and Paddy Two came up to him demanding a good night hug. That, as usual, the kids made an incredible racket when they were all brushing their teeth. Afterwards the junior assistants had to set the tables again for the next morning. No one mentioned what had happened before dinner, and Oliver gave Tycho a playful punch on the upper arm. Carol brought a load of new candles into the kitchen, and Josine stayed up with them. They talked about music.

I T GRADUALLY GOT QUIETER in the kitchen, on the stools surrounding the fridge. The candles had gone out, and they started speaking more and more softly—less often too. They were waiting for the word that any one of them might say any second now: "Good night." Tycho was no longer dreading having to walk beside Oliver down the cool hallways back to their supply closet. He was tired. He didn't want any more trouble. He could tell that Donna was looking at him, but he chose to ignore that for the time being. "All right, you guys, good night." He already heard the words in his head. Any moment now he'd be saying them, his tongue, his throat, his vocal cords were already gearing up.

But then they heard noises out in the hallway. Giggling and laughter and footsteps, way too fast, and way too unruly for this time of night. Singing, getting louder and closer, culminating in the sound of kitchen doors crashing open.

It was Gary, shouting: "Hiya, gals and pals! Y'all having fun?" Behind him were Director John and all the leaders who hadn't gone to bed yet. They were giddy with excitement as they grabbed the largest pot they could find, a kind of washtub big enough to fit a person, and filled it with lukewarm water. They'd brought shower gel, small bars of soap and shampoo, and they threw it all in there, whooping loudly. Carol, Josine, and the juniors got up and came closer. Tycho's curiosity won out over his exhaustion, and he went to the large pot with Oliver and Donna. Sherilynn joined the raucous leaders.

Suddenly everyone was calling for Gary. They started chanting his name, and he bowed and laughed and held up his hands: no, no, no. Tycho didn't know what had gotten into everyone. It couldn't be alcohol—drinking was forbidden on school grounds. The group started clapping, faster and faster, and cheering when they saw Gary's hands moving toward the edge of the pot. He looked for a moment like he was going to chicken out, laughing, but then Director John shouted "Go!" and Gary's hairy legs stepped in. Warm water sloshed onto the floor. People shrieked and jumped back. Gary lowered himself. His jeans slowly darkened. His T-shirt was still trying to resist, it started billowing out over the foam, but Gary was fully committed now and pushed it down into the water too. Applause. Director John high-fived him and everyone was howling with laughter. Gary got up, the sound of streaming water rising with him. He stepped out of the pot. His clothes were completely soaked through.

"Okay," John shouted, "who's next?"

"You!"

Director John stepped into the foam. More water sloshing over the rim. He was followed by several of the leaders. Everyone got thoroughly splashed; each time there was a round of applause.

Sherilynn shouted, "And now it's our little runaway's turn!"

Tycho flinched, though he tried not to let it show. He gave a halfhearted protest, already lifting one foot.

"But not by himself!" Gary shouted. Tycho looked up at him. Now what?

"Donna! Donna! He should get in there with Donna!"

Tycho looked for her eyes, for a nod of agreement. But then Carol said, "No! With Sherilynn!"

"Yeaaaah!" everyone yelled, and Sherilynn was pushed to the front. They had no choice. Together they took the first step. They wrapped their arms around each other so they wouldn't fall. Then they stepped into the pot with one leg each. They had to stick really close together—there was no other way. They sank into the foam, hugging each other.

Tycho couldn't tell whether this was fun or not— too much had gone on that day. As he got out of the pot, he felt his wet pants trying to pull him back down. He watched Oliver go in with Donna, followed by

Carol, and then no one. The air-conditioning in the kitchen was blowing cold air onto their wet clothes, so everyone retreated to the dorms, still giggling as they made their way down the hallway.

O LIVER AND TYCHO HAD to be quiet so they wouldn't wake any of the children. Drops of water plopped onto the floor. We'll mop up tomorrow, Tycho thought. They were standing in their closet, and Tycho closed the door to the classroom behind him.

Oliver snapped the light on.

Their eyes had to get used to the light; their pupils changed back from big to small. They looked at each other, realizing they both faced the same challenge. They had to take their pants off.

And they couldn't quite explain why, they weren't thinking about explanations, they weren't thinking at all—they both took a step forward, and then another, and another, and just like that their hands slid down and started searching for a button and a zipper—but not their own.

They undid each other's jeans and, without saying anything, let their hands wander to the hems of each other's T-shirts and underwear. They pulled one up, the other down, as if everything had to be peeled open from the center, like an eggshell. After a few seconds— but who was counting? Time no longer existed—they were standing there naked, their bodies almost touching.

Their fingers sparked. Slowly they slid their hands into and over each other's, and further, over their wrists, their elbows, upper arms, down each other's shoulder blades, down each other's backs. And every place they touched lit up, was transformed, became warmer and richer, and their mouths fit together perfectly and so did their tongues, they tasted fire and water, sea and sky, they moved closer together and clasped their hands around each other's lower backs.

E VERY NOW AND THEN one of them would lift the other up, as if trying to hoist him into his heart.

And then the night began. Liftoff.

WHEN TYCHO WOKE UP the next morning, he saw an ear. He looked at it and thought to himself: I didn't know an ear could be so beautiful. He stuck his tongue out a little and licked the downy hairs along its edge. The ear moved—a slight jerk, then another, and Oliver woke up. Tycho noticed his arm was hurting. Oliver had been lying on top of it all night. He carefully tried to get it out, but that caused Oliver to roll over onto his side, facing him. Oliver tried to say something, his voice still hoarse with sleep, but nothing came out. They both laughed. It occurred to Tycho that from up close it might be hard to tell whether he was smiling or grimacing, so he puckered his lips and kissed straight ahead of him. Three, four times.

"D'you think this is what they mean by 'friendship that crosses borders'?" Oliver seemed to have gotten his voice back.

"I hope so," Tycho said. He chuckled and brushed a strand of hair from Oliver's face.

"I hope so too," Oliver said. "What time is it?"

He lifted his body up slightly. The sheet slipped off his chest, as if he were a statue still to be unveiled. He leaned over Tycho, reaching for the watch that he'd dropped onto the floor the previous night. He looked at it and jumped up.

"Shit! I was supposed to go jogging with some of the kids!" He flipped back the sheet and swung his legs off the bed, his naked torso brushing past Tycho.

Tycho watched Oliver begin to get dressed. He propped Oliver's pillow behind his back and watched him tug on his boxer shorts and sweatpants. He saw Oliver put his bare feet into his sneakers and bend his knees to tie his shoelaces. He saw Oliver walk over to the wardrobe, rummage around, find a T-shirt, and shake it out. But before he put his head through the neck, the door to the classroom opened slightly. One of the children poked his head around the corner and asked softly, "Oliver, you come?"

"One second!" Oliver shouted. "Have you heard of knocking?" He resolutely pushed the door shut again. He pulled on his T-shirt and gave Tycho a half-apologetic look.

"They don't need to know."

Tycho nodded.

Oliver said, "I guess I should go."

He grabbed the door handle, then hesitated and turned around again. He walked back over to Tycho and bent down for a brief kiss. I guess that's what people do in this situation, Tycho thought, feeling surprised all the same.

OLIVER WAS GONE. HE'D closed the door behind him. Tycho was still in bed. He felt his body thrumming with contentment—completely relaxed, as if it had finally arrived somewhere it had wanted to go for a long time. But his mind, which for hours had believed itself to be out of a job—sidelined, just like that—suddenly pushed back. Who was allowed to know about this? It helpfully listed the pros and cons: this was so private, no one in the entire Little World needed to know, and besides, how would the entire Little World react? But what about Donna? Donna would be able to tell. She'd seen this coming. She'd been right.

And all the others? How could you hide that you'd grown, that you'd become more complete? His skin, his posture, his hands, everything about him would say it out loud—to anyone who was listening. He'd need to look again at his reflection in the mirror later, look himself in the eyes, but he already knew they'd give him away. You couldn't hide something so alive.

THEY SHOULD BE LEFT alone, the two of them, just for a little while. He got out of bed. All that thinking had gotten his body fired up again, but this time it was his head that decided not to worry. He looked for the pants he'd kicked off the previous night and heard something inside of him begin to sing. A new, happy-go-lucky song: "Da da da so what?" He hummed along. So what to his socks and so what to his sleeping bag and so what to the whole room. He did a spontaneous drum solo on Oliver's mattress, climbed up onto the top bunk, spread his arms, and tried to take flight, even though the floor was much too close to float in the air for even just a moment. Crash! Landed. "Da da da so what?"

He started composing a message to his parents in his head. He'd send it off to Southampton this afternoon: *Mom, Dad, you'll never guess what happened.* He didn't know how to go on from there. *I'm happy.* (As long as they knew that, he thought, that was the most important part.) *Sorry if that sounds kind of stupid, but it's true.* And then what? *X, Tycho.*

OLIVER CAME IN. HE was done jogging and his face was red. "Time for breakfast!" Tycho nodded and got up, throwing a towel at Oliver, who pulled off his T-shirt and said, "I thought about it. Let's keep it just between us."

So what? Tycho thought, and he said, "If that's what you want. But I'm sure Donna will know."

He brought his hand to Oliver's face and rubbed a small streak of sweat off his temple.

"Hm. I guess that's okay," Oliver said. His lips didn't close after that last sound—the "ay" hung in midair, beckoning silently. Tycho's lips also made a silent "ay." He followed his lips—which in turn were following Oliver's lips.

After some time, Oliver pulled away. He unlaced his hands from behind Tycho's back and put them on his shoulders—a split-second transformation from boyfriend back to best friend—and said, "Ready for normal life?"

"I'm capable of anything now!" Tycho said.

Oliver quickly changed his shirt and Tycho put the pillows back in place.

Then they made their way from the supply closet through the dorm, the hallway, and the auditorium, into the kitchen.

T HE WHOLE WORLD HAS transformed, Tycho thought to himself, as he poured out cornflakes and handed out cups of yogurt. Everyone seemed so cheerful. So friendly. So beautiful. There was humming and singing, all the leaders were cracking jokes, all the girls were laughing happily. Someone had tidied up the kitchen. The big pot had been rinsed out, the floor had been mopped, and there were no suds left anywhere. The contents of the trash can were the only reminder of the previous evening: shampoo bottles and dented cans of Diet Coke.

"You're singing," Donna said.

"Am I?"

"Has something good happened, by any chance?"

"Maybe!" Tycho said, and he loaded a basket full of dirty silverware into the dishwasher, grinning.

D URING THOSE FIRST FEW days, Tycho could handle anything. Even during the day. His energy and attention, his motivation, his good mood— it seemed as if love was keeping all his reserves stocked up. Tycho was a kite soaring high in the sky. And whether he was beneath the clouds of the camp, or bathed in the brilliant blue of everything to do with Oliver—he had the wind at his back.

What counted were the evenings. And the nights. The times when Oliver and Tycho were together. When they could talk without feeling like they were saying lines, playing characters that were only semi-real at this point. They had to whisper—half the camp was asleep behind the thin door—so they used as few words as possible: a brief summary of their day, things of immediate relevance (are you comfortable, what time is it, I still have chocolate, are you asleep), and every now and then they would talk about how they'd ended up here. Oliver told Tycho how happy it had made him when he'd spotted Tycho's T-shirt at Amsterdam airport. "So it wasn't really about Ajax?" Tycho asked. "No. Well, it was about Ajax *and* about you." And

Tycho told Oliver about the river, the streaming river down his face, his narrow chest, his stomach . . .

That's how Tycho would remember it later: all those first nights began with words that eventually ran out, followed by feeling each other's skin. Then the touching that slowly gave way to a sensation of warm snow, of melting. Until finally all that remained of the two of them was someone who was Tycho-and-Oliver both: a third body. A third body that made them both think, feel, and know the same things. That fell asleep and woke up again the next day, a hand here—whose hand?—and a leg there, a foot, a toe. A third body that ultimately morphed back into Tycho and Oliver again, but only after they'd said "goeiemorgen" and "god morn."

THE DAYS AND NIGHTS were packed, but every now and then Tycho found a little gap to reflect on what was going on. In those moments he understood that he wasn't just in love. That there were other feelings involved that rose up from time to time, in quiet moments.

For example, sometimes he felt amazed when it hit him that it had only been eleven, twelve, thirteen days since he and Oliver first met—though he was sure that he knew him. And yet there had to be a thousand tidbits, slivers of information, things about the past, that they didn't know about each other. That's when jealousy would kick in. He'd feel jealous of everyone who'd known Oliver all his life. His classmates, who'd gotten to spend lunch breaks with him, bitch with him about horrible teachers and difficult exams. Who'd gone to his graduation party. His football friends, who may have practiced with him, played with him, showered, won or lost with him a hundred times. His neighbors, who'd gone to the local ski jumping festival with him. He'd feel jealous of Oliver's family, who knew what he'd been like as a little boy, at three, five, nine years old. His mother, and his father.

His girlfriends. Girlfriends?

No, there hadn't been any, not really, Oliver said.

"'Not really'?" Tycho asked.

"No," Oliver said.

And Tycho breathed a sigh of relief, though he still wanted to know everything—what, when, how often. And he told Oliver about Nina—oh, Nina, what would she say if she knew that . . . ?—but he didn't really seem to care.

"Why doesn't it bother you?" Tycho asked.

"Dunno," Oliver said. "Do you think about her a lot?"

"Not really," Tycho said.

"Well, that's why," Oliver said.

And then that reply would kindle doubt in Tycho

again. How could Oliver not be jealous? Did he maybe love Oliver more than Oliver loved him? That kind of nonsense.

Sometimes Tycho thought about his parents. He wished they knew. He didn't want to tell them, but he wanted them to know. He wanted to fast-forward past all of it: the news, their reaction, their concern. Eventually they'd understand and they'd be happy, because their son was happy and happiness is infectious. But first everything would have to be complicated. First he'd have to say what he felt—and he didn't do that very often.

He decided to write it down after all. During the next free period he took a deep breath, deleted his previous draft, and started over, then erased that too and typed another message. *Hi Mom, hi Dad. So much has changed. I'm happy. I met someone here. It's the boy I told you about before. His name is Oliver Kjelsberg, and he's from Norway. I wish you could meet him. I feel like I've known him for ages. Because of him everything is fantastic. It's the real thing. It's a little strange, of course, but it's the real thing, like I said. Don't worry—I'm doing great, better than ever. X, Tycho.*

IIe read it through and felt like he'd gone about it all wrong, but he didn't know how else to say it. And he was late for his shift at the camp store. He sent it . . . No, wait! He didn't send it quite yet.

A T THE END OF the second week, they were back at the school entrance—the staff, the leaders, and the junior assistants—shaking hands, shouting "bye, take care, see you tomorrow," waving, jumping around. They watched the host parents drive away. One by one the Buicks, the Mercs, and the Dodges turned their backs on them. They saw the kids looking out from the backseats, receding picture frames on an asphalt dresser.

The third weekend had begun, which meant the kids were going off to their next host families. The leaders had the weekend to themselves to catch their breath, rest up, and evaluate how things had gone so far.

There they were. Carol saw that everyone was at a bit of a loss. It was so empty all of a sudden, so quiet without the kids' voices, so she shouted "Hugging line!" She grabbed Tycho, and then Adele and Yoshi and Josine, and pulled them into a line. "Come on, come on!" Moments later, there they were, all standing side by side, waiting to see what was going to happen next.

Carol, short and small, spread her arms and hugged Tycho. The others applauded. Tycho felt her breasts pressing against his body. It was hot, their T-shirts clung together, but he understood what he was supposed to do. When Carol moved on to hug Adcle, and then Yoshi, he had to follow her. He hugged Adele.

Tycho made his way down the line. He hugged Yoshi, happy and welcoming; Josine, tentative, friendly; Brahim, so broad and warm; and then all the others, up to and including Director John, who practically crushed everyone out of sheer gratitude—when he put his arms around you it was like he was trying to impress the World Wrestling Federation with his muscle strength.

The last person in the line was Oliver. Tycho had embraced the fifteen others in a smooth hugging rhythm, the camp director's burly body the center of gravity. Now he was face-to-face with his friend, his boyfriend. They looked at each other.

In that moment a button must have been pushed—*click!*—in Tycho's brain, in the part of his brain that converted Oliver's gaze into an image—*Memory, Record, Slow Motion*—because later on he'd be able to replay the next few seconds endlessly. As many times as he wanted.

R EWIND, PLAY: OLIVER'S GREEN eyes catching his own: what do we do now, how should we hug each other, have we forgotten how two cool junior assistants are supposed to do that? Oliver's nod, the small downward tilt of his chin, his head, his eyelids: come on, let's get this over with. Raising their arms, their left arms high, their right arms low, yes, it fits; one chest against the other, their hearts giving each other a quick wink, and their heads ear to ear—the scent of shampoo and skin. The scent of night.

Tycho is already pulling back, he takes a step backwards, his arms let go and fall down alongside his body, but then look! Oliver's left arm lets go, while the right—look!—moves upwards, the fingers open up—and brush against Tycho's left cheek.

Tycho looks up at Oliver in surprise, and Oliver's face cracks into a grin. Oliver looks him in the eyes, Tycho is startled and turns away and sees that Director John is staring straight at Oliver's hand. And Tycho feels what Director John is seeing—that what Oliver's hand is doing isn't rubbing but stroking, the way you stroke a lover.

End of fragment.

TYCHO GREW HOT WITH confusion: Oliver's hand, Director John's look, the pleasant sensation of Oliver's touch, the jolt of fear . . . Had his own "da da da so what" and Oliver's misgivings traded places? Switched bodies?

He didn't get the chance to work out what was going on, because it was time for Coca-Cola and their first brief staff meeting. "To the leaders' room!" Director John said.

The conference table felt blissfully cool against Tycho's forearms. Maybe that's what helped shake things into order in his head and made him decide to pay attention. He leaned into the meeting. Oliver was sitting three, four chairs down from him. Tycho saw his hands and a pen, his fingers. Don't go there.

"I want you guys to write down," Director John said, "what's going well and what isn't. Take a minute to think about it, be honest and help us figure out where there's room for improvement. We'll discuss the results tomorrow afternoon, when we get back from Chattanooga."

They were going on a trip. They were driving down to Chattanooga in the air-conditioned minivans, to a small hotel, and then "Tonight we'll go dancing."

Tycho couldn't come up with anything to write down. He wanted to get out of there, run around, but he had to say something, so he wrote "Everything is great" in big letters and slid the piece of paper over to Carol.

"Your face was so close," Oliver said, "and then it just happened. That's okay, right?"

"Yeah, it's okay," Tycho said. "But I thought you wanted to keep it just between us."

"Jeez, I don't know, I mean . . . Can't we just leave?"

"Leave?"

"I dunno . . . get out of here, just the two of us?"

"Yes!" Tycho all but leapt to his feet.

"Gimme those bags!" Gary came in, holding out a hairy arm. "Hurry up, it's time to go!"

AFTER HOURS IN THE vans, they turned in to the driveway of the hotel. "Here's your key. We're meeting in the lobby in forty-five minutes." They headed off to their rooms in pairs, dragging their luggage along with them.

Oliver and Tycho had room number 20. Green wall-to-wall carpeting, a television set, yellow wallpaper with bits of forest on it, two bedside lamps with broken lampshades and, in the middle of the room, a double bed, as wide as the sky. A bed for husbands.

"We can push them apart," Tycho said, "if we want."

He lifted up the heavy duvet to show that there were actually two twin beds.

"But we don't want," Oliver said.

He sat down on the bed and tugged on Tycho's T-shirt, so that Tycho fell down next to him, curling into his left arm, which he was offering as a backrest, with the rest of him as the chair. They turned toward each other. Their noses touched, and Tycho said, "A shame we were in different vans."

"A real shame."

Oliver started kissing his ear. His lips glided over Tycho's temple, his neck, his chin, the space underneath his lips. Tycho shifted his head half an inch, until his lips met Oliver's. Locked together.

They scooched up the bed and pushed their pillows together.

Tycho spotted a box hanging on the wall. He said, "Do you have any change?"

"What?"

"Change. There's some kind of box by the bed. A machine."

Oliver fished a coin out of his pocket. Tycho inserted it into the slot and pushed a button. Suddenly the right side of the bed started vibrating.

"A *massaging* bed!" Tycho cried, and he flipped Oliver upside down and threw himself on top of him.

A KNOCK. TYCHO GOT up to open the door. Director John. "Everything all right here? I see you guys found the massage button." His eyes darted around the room, as if he was looking for something. He glanced over at Oliver, who'd gotten up too.

"You like the room?"

"Yeah," Oliver said, but suddenly Tycho noticed what Director John had probably noticed too: the two pillows pushed together, and in the sheets on one side of the bed, the outline of two boys. Not one, no, clearly two—two boy-imprints that were still buzzing, as the machine hadn't run out yet.

"All right then. I'll see you in a bit."

THEY'D CLOSED THE DOOR behind Director John. There they were, still standing next to the bed, which was now massaging the air.

Tycho said, "He definitely saw it this time."

"So be it." Oliver shrugged.

"You don't care?" Tycho asked.

"No. Do you?"

"Um, no. I don't think so. Have you been in touch with your mother? I have. Almost."

"I haven't. She's in Africa. On safari, remember? She probably has no signal out there anyway."

Oliver pulled another coin out of his pocket. "Another ride?"

CHATTANOOGA TURNED OUT TO be a city filled with shopping streets. They all strolled along, stopping at practically every store because one or another of the leaders wanted to check it out. Oliver and Tycho didn't buy anything. They walked along, more or less side by side. Tycho was swinging his arms. In his mind he'd already pushed an arm out several times and let it drift to the side—what do you know, we're holding hands—but no, he managed to resist that magnetic field.

But he couldn't stop what was going on inside his head: he could feel how with every swing of his arms something new, something unfamiliar, something rebellious was rising up inside him. He felt how, with every step, one thought was pressing forward more and more, like a quarter being carefully inserted into one of those coin pushers at the fun fair—until it drops. Wait a minute, he thought, why, why not? If two leaders can be all over each other, then why can't we?

Suddenly he understood Oliver. They should be brave—no, not brave, they should just be themselves, stop thinking about it, just do it!

They were standing in front of a souvenir shop. Right here, he thought, we could maybe take each other's hand . . . slip an arm around each other's waist . . . maybe another caress . . . But then someone said, "Right! It's time to go! Everyone over here, we're leaving!"

D IRECTOR JOHN AND GARY were excited. "You're gonna have the perfect night out!" They were standing in front of a barbecue joint looking at the entrance. Flashing lights, signs saying, ICE COLD BEER, LIVE PERFORMANCES, and thick wooden double doors.

They headed toward them and the others followed suit. They went inside, down a hallway and through a set of saloon doors, which everyone held open for each other and which pointed, like two wooden arrows, toward a large room with huge plants, barbecue pits, extractor hoods, tables, and a stage with a dance floor. Right in the middle of that stage stood a double bass, a spotlight shining down on it.

The group had come to a halt, because Director John was negotiating a package deal for seventeen with someone behind the bar. Tycho read the text on the posters on the wall: THE MARC MCKINLEY BLUEGRASS BAND. Oliver was looking over Tycho's shoulder. They waited. They asked each other what bluegrass was. They said they didn't know. So they waited.

But suddenly something started quivering inside the two of them. Why? Because of what? It was as if it had dawned on them that they were together, very close together, right in the middle of everyone else. Tycho noticed his breath quickening, and he tried to exhale in the same moments that he could feel Oliver blowing air onto his neck. Once, twice, three times. Until it stopped. Oliver started whispering. He said, "I want to sit next to you tonight," and briefly put his hand on Tycho's hip. A storm of excitement blew through Tycho, as if that touch, those fingers, had activated something, set something in motion, turned up the glowing in his cheeks, started the thumping in his throat, sent goose bumps over his whole body. He tilted his head back and slowly moved it to the side. His heart was pounding. Everyone could see his bare throat, could see him swallowing. He tilted farther back toward Oliver and whispered "Jeg elsker deg" into his ear.

"I love you too," Oliver murmured and slid around until he was in front of Tycho. He let his arm and his hand dangle down and, in passing, he—accidentally, invisible to everyone else—brushed it against Tycho's crotch.

The whole evening was charged with electricity. Ordering sweet tea, a beer when the staff wasn't watching, walking back and forth to the bar to get meat and onions, the barbecuing itself, the oil and the grill and the hot coal, the conversation—Oliver and Tycho were sitting next to each other, but Donna was there too, and Carol and Adele—the things they talked about and the words they said, all of it was electric, even just speaking in English instead of Dutch— "wow" and "great" and "sure" and "wonderful."

And then there was the music. The Marc McKinley Bluegrass Band started playing when they'd almost finished dessert. Tanned men wearing cowboy hats, Western shirts, and jeans, all five of them dressed the same—a guitarist, someone playing the mandolin, someone with a banjo, someone on bass. And the singer: Marc McKinley himself. "So nice to be here folks—with you, tonight—it's Saturday—Saturday night—the perfect time for a little dancing—but before all that—we'll get into the spirit—with some fine old tunes—some happy tunes—so on behalf of me and all the band—enjoy the show!" And over the "ow" in "show" the guitar kicked in, playing the first notes of the first song.

It was as if they were rockets launching up into the sky—that's how much fire and energy these old men were giving off. Tycho had never heard this kind of music before. Music? It was like heat with a voice. The superfast rhythms and the explosions of banjo were like the waves of heat coming off the barbecue, except turned into sound. Pleasant waves. Tycho was glowing. From the fire, the wood, the ribs, the coleslaw, and the shining faces of his campmates, his friends—yes, his *friends*—and Oliver, his Oliver, those green eyes (which saw him) and that small, straight nose (which tonight he would feel pressed against his own), that beautiful mouth (which tonight . . .)—all of that, it was all those things taken together, heightened, deepened by the music, as if the music was lifting every feeling, every sensation, to the next level—*Having fun, folks? Having fun!*

L ATER THAT NIGHT, THEY finally got around to dancing. Square dancing. Everyone was on the dance floor—Gary had corralled them over there —arranged into some sort of geometric figure, arms linked with the person on either side of them. McKinley was giving directions. The double bass and the banjo were playing, and they had to split up into pairs and touch hands with the couple across from them ("Up to the middle and back!" Marc shouted) and then pass around each other back-to-back ("Go forward again and do-si-do!"). The rhythm took care of the rest.

Tycho did as he was told, letting it all happen, swinging around arm in arm with an elderly lady. She smiled at him and he smiled back. Another beer? Another beer! And would the Marc McKinley Bluegrass Band be playing an encore? Sure, why not—and the whole camp gathered in a circle, arms around each other's shoulders, Tycho gesturing at Oliver, come on, come stand next to me. Booing because the band had left the stage, and then, later, another circle, right in the middle of the dance floor, holding hands, right arm over left, *learn a lesson, make a friend.*

T HE DRIVE BACK TO the hotel. The two of them going back up to their room. The sky-wide bed. And Oliver saying, "Let them talk—let's make bluegrass love . . ."

Let them talk? Oh yeah, there'd been the banging on the door, the shouting, "All right, guys . . . have a ball!" followed by loud laughter.

And then Oliver saying, "Let them talk—let's make bluegrass love . . ."

Wow, this is the first time we didn't have to set the table," Donna laughed. The four of them were sitting together. Tycho wasn't that hungry—he just ate a pancake with maple syrup. Sherilynn wanted cornflakes, Donna wanted bread. Oliver wasn't eating anything. He kept up the conversation. He said he'd already watched TV and there were more than forty channels. He'd even found a Swedish church service. And he'd watched a few minutes of a baseball game.

"And what about you?" Sherilynn suddenly asked Tycho. "Did you watch TV too, by any chance?" There was an odd sharpness to her voice, and Tycho glanced up at her before answering. She looked back at him with hard eyes, though she pulled her mouth into a smile.

"I took a shower."

"You took a *shower*! Oh, and what about you, Oliver, did you take a shower too this morning?"

Oliver started laughing. "Yes, I took a shower too, right after watching TV. Happy?"

Sherilynn shrugged. "I thought maybe you guys got in the shower together."

"No," Oliver said, "we didn't. But we might have."

Carol asked if she could join their table. "Girls," she asked Sherilynn and Donna, "Did you sleep well?"

"Sure, great," Sherilynn said. Her voice sounded normal again.

"And you guys?" Carol said, turning to Oliver and Tycho. "How was your night?"

Tycho wondered if something was up. She looked so serious. "Yeah, fine," Oliver said.

"What about yours?" Tycho said.

"Oh, fine, just a little short. John wanted to have a quick meeting."

"What, this morning?"

"What about?"

That last question came from Sherilynn.

"It's not important," Carol said. "By the way, we're leaving at eleven, so make sure your bags are packed on time. And prepare some lunch. I've got paper bags. Oh, and we'll be in the same vans on the way back."

THEY WERE BACK AT the camp and Tycho thought: It's like it got ten degrees hotter in just one day. He ran back and forth getting suitcases, backpacks, and duffel bags out of the vans. He was sweating. There was a thermostat hanging from the school building, but it gave the temperature in Fahrenheit. How much was that in Celsius?

Someone placed a hand over his shoulder—so warm! Tycho turned around in a single motion and saw the camp director. "Tycho," Director John said, mispronouncing his name—"tie" instead of "tee." "Can I have a quick word?"

"Sure," Tycho said hesitantly, surprised. "But what about the luggage?"

"The luggage . . ." the camp director said. "We'll take care of that later. First we need to talk."

How strange, Tycho thought. What was there to discuss? Last night, had he . . . ? Bluegrass love! Was it about the pounding on the door? Where was Oliver? Or did Director John want to talk about something to do with his junior assistant duties? A private evaluation? Was someone sick? Maybe Gitte from Denmark? Did he want Tycho to take over one of the delegations?

Director John strode off and Tycho followed along behind him. They stopped in front of the staff room— the camp director held the door open for Tycho. That was when he understood: this wasn't a meeting about sick leaders, kitchen duty, or the Little World T-shirts in the juniors' camp shop being way too expensive.

Inside, on a chair in front of the desk, sat Oliver. "Hey," Tycho said. Shit. That sounded way too meek. Too hoarse. Too intimidated.

"Hi," Oliver said, giving him a reassuring smile.

"Take a seat," said Director John.

Tycho picked a chair next to Oliver. The camp director sat down in the swivel chair behind the desk. He took off his cap. Clicked a pen. Crossed his arms. Heaved a deep sigh.

"This isn't going to be an easy conversation," he began. "I've been a part of seven Little World camps. I've been a participant and I've been a junior assistant. I was a delegation leader twice, and this is my third year as camp director. In each of those camps, I've watched people fall in love. In fact, I didn't just watch it happen—I met the woman I'm now married to in France, where she was the leader of the Philippine delegation. So I don't want you to think I don't get how this sort of thing happens. You're far away from home, you feel free, anything's possible, and suddenly it hits you. We've seen it in this camp, too. But now I understand that—how shall I put it—the two of you have found each other. Am I right?"

Tycho glanced at Oliver, who didn't react.

"Come on," said Director John. "I see the way you act around each other, and last night we all saw you guys on the dance floor."

Tycho thought: I have to say something, and then he said: "Well, what does it matter?"

"Right," Director John said. "What does it matter? . . . Wow, this is new to me." He rubbed his hands over his face from top to bottom, pausing half-way down. He peered at Tycho over the tips of his fingers, just for a moment. The boss figuring out his next move. Then he let them slide on down his cheeks. They ended up clasped together, as if in prayer, his fingertips touching his lips and his nose. They stayed that way for five or six seconds. Then they flew apart and landed flat on the desk. Bam. No more hand choreography. Back to words. "I have a friend who's gay."

Out of the corner of his eye Tycho saw Oliver moving. Shifting his foot. Shifting in his seat.

"So that's not the issue. The Little World Organization is open-minded. We don't close our hearts to minorities—no one is excluded based on their ethnicity or sexual orientation . . ." Tycho wanted to stop listening. Stop, he thought. Stop. He looked at Oliver, who was staring out the window. Was he smiling?

". . . but we're not here alone. We also have to think of our fellow campers. And I'm sure you understand that not everyone will find it as easy to accept your— what should I call it?—*relationship*, as we do. There may be people in this camp who have a hard time with it. We have to consider them too. I'm sure you'll agree. And that's why I'm asking you to think about what I'm saying. Talk to each other about it. I can't tell you what to do—you're both eighteen, after all—but maybe you guys could cool it a little. Be a little less obvious."

Chair legs scraping the floor. Oliver got up and walked out of the room.

The camp director looked up and said, "I wasn't finished," but Oliver was gone.

Tycho thought: Now what? What do I do? He rose to his feet too. He thought: I need to go after him, but Director John grabbed his arm and stopped him. Tycho let himself be stopped. Director John said, "Just let him be—he needs time. You're a smart boy, I like you. You know what's best for him, and for you. And maybe you need to give him a nudge in the right direction. He's gotten into some scrapes before. With Sherilynn for example. I'm sure you know about that. But you can help your friend, and you will—I'm sure of it. Carol tells me you can handle it. She has a very high opinion of you, you know."

All Tycho could do was give a taut nod and leave.

T YCHO WENT AND LOOKED for Oliver. He wasn't in their supply closet, he wasn't in the kitchen, and he wasn't in the leaders' room. Tycho walked and thought and searched. The common room? No—he saw Carol, poring over the evaluation forms with Gary. Carol looked up at him. He didn't ask her anything. *She has a very high opinion of you, you know.*

He went outside. He saw movement on the field.

Four people with their shirts off. Four torsos. Oliver and Gary and Brahim and Yoshi. They were playing football and Oliver was standing in the goal. Tycho headed over. Oliver saw him and shouted, "Wanna join in?"

No, Tycho thought, no. Too hot. Too much to think about. He shook his head.

"Okay!" Oliver shouted, preparing to defend. He motioned for Yoshi to shoot, beckoning with the fingers of his right hand: come on, come on, go for it.

Tycho sat down under a tree to think. I'm experiencing something, he thought. An adventure. A movie in 3-D. I'm the protagonist. I'm looking at myself. I need to do something. I need to have an opinion. I have to figure out how I feel about Director John. I have to figure out if it's true what he said. I have to not be thrown by those words. I have to turn them into new words. Words that don't make me think of something else, something I'm not.

He looked at Oliver. We have to be together, he thought. We have to take each other by the hand, take a running start, and dive into the ocean. Break the surface together. Operate together. "Scalpel," I'll shout, and then he'll bring me what I need. "Oxygen!" he'll shout, and I'll be ready.

We should have gone over to the staff room together. We should have walked out together too. And when

one of us said something, the other should have nodded. From now on we have to talk as one. Finish each
other's sentences.

Oliver dove after the ball, punching it away with
all his might.

The ball rocketed across the mouth of the goal,
missing the far post, flying over the line and out of
play. Oliver got up to get it, and so did Tycho. They
both made a beeline for the ball. When they got to it,
Tycho said, "Are you mad at me?"

"What? Of course not! Why?" Oliver asked.

"I wanted to walk out with you, but he stopped me."

"Oh, don't worry about that. Did you see that
save?"

"Yeah—you were great. Let's talk about this later?"

"Yeah. Later."

Tycho headed back inside, looking over his shoulder at Oliver. The lines of his body shone with sweat.
He snatched balls out of the air, hanging in the netting for a brief moment like a comet with a tail. The
three others looked so awkward and lumbering next
to him! Gary, huffing and red all over, Brahim with
his chest hair, as if someone had doodled on his body,
Yoshi, lean and tall and as cheerful as ever. But in the
midst of them, standing and sprinting, dribbling and
falling, and so exactly as he should be—as if the air
was inventing perfect shapes for him and he constantly,

dazzlingly, filled in those shapes—was Oliver. No, the camp director had it all wrong. There was nothing Oliver needed to be helped with. There was nothing at all. There was sun, there was a tree, and there was a view.

H E HEARD DONNA SHOUTING. She was waving. She came running over to Tycho. She crouched down in front of him, grabbed his elbows, and panted, "Everyone's talking about it!" She let go and dropped onto the ground. She said they'd come and given her the third degree, but she hadn't told them anything. Ask Tycho, ask Oliver, she'd said. But a little later, in the leaders' room, she'd overheard them all talking about it. One person had shrieked in surprise and another had shrugged her shoulders. One person had mumbled something and another had gotten grumpy. Adele hadn't reacted, but Gary, who'd been moving tables around with the camp director, had made a weird joke. People had laughed, and that was when she'd run off to find him.

Tycho listened. He listened to Donna, but his eyes wandered down, to Donna's breasts. They seemed bigger and rounder than Nina's pointy ones. He wished he knew why he liked Oliver's flat chest better. Was it because a boy's chest was more modest somehow, more vulnerable? And girls' breasts too out there, too in-your-face? The things you liked . . . did you come to like them over time? Or were you born with a preference?

Donna said, "Sorry, but I thought you'd want to know." She looked at him and Tycho looked back at her and he realized just in time that he was supposed to say something. He didn't want to. Suddenly he was sick of talking about him and Oliver. Wasn't there something else they could talk about?

"Oh, of course!" he said. "Thank you. You have to keep me updated. But tell me more about your brother."

Donna raised her eyebrows, but then she started talking. She loved him. He was her older brother and, oh, she just adored him. Whenever she had a problem or a weird question or wanted to complain about school, he'd tell her to sit down and he'd drop everything he was doing and let her talk until she got sick of herself. He lived in an apartment in the city and she always went there to see him. And he wasn't married and he didn't have a girlfriend because he was gay. So yeah. That was the story. And that would all be just fine if he didn't have a problem with it. But he did. No one was allowed to know. Not at his job, not in church, not at home. Half of his life was a giant secret. Donna knew. She saw how he went quiet when people asked certain questions and how he made every effort to avoid the subject. And she didn't know what to do.

But with them, with him and Oliver, everything seemed to be going so well, and she didn't want everyone to know and for everyone to have an opinion about it and for him and Oliver to . . . Shh, Tycho wanted to say, shh, it's okay, but suddenly he remembered Sherilynn. "You haven't mentioned Sherilynn yet."

A bitter little laugh. "I'm afraid she's the one who's spreading the news."

THE FOOTBALL GAME WAS over. Oliver went up to them. The others were looking for their T-shirts.

"The best thing you can do is sweat!" Oliver said. Tycho laughed. And finally Donna laughed too.

She looked at her watch and got up. "It's almost three o'clock. The meeting's about to start."

"I have to go change first," Oliver said. "Are you coming?"

As they walked over to the boys' dorm, Tycho talked a mile a minute to try and catch Oliver up. He started by telling him everything he'd realized and everything he'd heard. But then doubts and speculations reared up, what if this and suppose that—

"Stop!" Oliver said.

He was tying his shoelaces. He looked up and said, "Listen! I don't want to be gay. At least not like that. I'm just Oliver Kjelsberg from Norway. That's all. And

Tycho Zeling from the Netherlands is the person I want to be with, and even if I spend every minute of my life with you, I don't want anyone to bitch and moan about it—and if they do, they better watch out, because I know a few ways to knock that crap right out of their heads!"

Oliver the gangster. Tycho hadn't seem him like this before. He chuckled.

"Shall we?" Oliver said, grinning.

"Yes," Tycho said, smiling too.

"And maybe this is our chance," Oliver said, straightening the bows of his shoelaces.

T HE FIFTEEN MINUTES THAT followed were like the premiere of a strange play. *Watching the Boys*, it might have been called. Oliver and Tycho enter stage left. The door is open, so a lot of movements have already been edited out (door handle, fingers, pushing, hinges squealing, swinging open). Then they enter the room. First Tycho and then Oliver, with a relaxed gait and a distance of, let's say, fifteen inches between them. The end point of their journey—the conference table. They survey the room. Scattered throughout the space are people. Their main preoccupation: observing. But each in their own way—a sidelong glance, a peek out of the corner of their eye, a furtive once-over, and even a wide-eyed stare—all of which comes to an abrupt halt when the camp director picks up his papers and taps on the table. Everyone grabs a pen and goes to find a chair, but only after they've all registered the fact that the boys have sat down right in the center. Next to each other.

Carol is sitting with Gary. Gary is sitting with Director John. Donna has pulled up a chair next to Tycho, and Brahim is sitting with Oliver. Both of them are staring at Josine's hands, straight across from them. Sherilynn walks in and searches out a seat at the end of the table. People glance over at her, and then from her to Oliver and Tycho, who pretend not to notice, but then Director John puts his palms flat on the table and coughs. All eyes turn toward his mouth.

TYCHO NO LONGER HEARD violins screeching in the air. No vibrato, no pizzicato. He'd resolved to give nothing away, he'd decided he could handle anything. But even if you don't want to look at it or listen to it, turmoil all around you has a way of seeping into your body. How? Through your skin, your pores? It buzzes around your head like a swarm of mosquitoes. Like the sound of saws whining—impossible to ignore. He breathed out again.

He looked around the conference table and thought: There's something reassuring about sitting at a table together, about hearing the director open the meeting, about his American twang. But what did Oliver mean when he said, *Maybe this is our chance?*

Thankfully he didn't need to speak. The meeting was about the flag ceremony, about how to decide who was hoisting the flag. About the hamburger surplus at dinnertime. About bedtime. About little things. He saw that Oliver was using the meeting to doodle. He was drawing a figure with fingers that were a little too short, a belly that was a little too fat, and a baseball cap that was a little too big. And suddenly—Tycho had no idea what had gotten into his head, his arm, his fingers—he leaned over and knocked the pencil out of Oliver's hand. It skittered across the table and landed in Gary's lap. "Brother Jacob" Gary.

Everyone looked up.

The camp director stopped in midsentence, and Gary pushed the pen back toward Oliver.

Director John hesitantly resumed his story. The meeting went on, but now Oliver was trying to rip up Tycho's piece of paper from under the table. When he realized what Oliver was doing, Tycho curled his body into a bulwark. Oliver's arm was trapped. "Shit!" he said in a half-loud whisper.

Again the camp director fell silent. Again all eyes were on them.

Director John took a deep breath and said that he didn't want to have to stop again. And especially not for foul language. Tycho said, "I'm sorry," but the last syllable of his "sorry" was smothered by a giggle, because Oliver was squeezing him between the ribs. "I'm sorry," he said again, this time managing to get the whole word out.

Frowns.

Troubled looks.

"Right, as I was saying . . ." Director John said.

Tycho turned his attention to Yoshi rather than Oliver. Yoshi was listening and playing with his pen. He threw it into the air, where it flipped one or two somersaults before he caught it again. An odd sight. Don't laugh. Yoshi was listening. Yoshi's hands had stopped moving now, and his head began to droop to his chest. Don't laugh, Tycho. Yoshi's eyes were closing—or were they? Don't laugh, Tycho. He couldn't hold it in any longer—he cracked up. Loudly, and right as one of the leaders was making an impassioned plea about something. Director John slammed his hand down on the table, but Carol shoved her chair back and said she was taking the junior assistants aside for a separate evaluation.

"Now!"

I DON'T FEEL LIKE TALKING," Oliver said. Sherilynn gave him a dirty look. Carol shook her head. Donna looked from left to right, at a loss. Tycho was curious. On their way to the kitchen—Carol resolutely marching on ahead—Oliver had briefly brushed his fingers down Tycho's back. Then they had sat down, on stools by the fridge. Hands in their laps—those hands didn't know where to go from here either.

Tycho stopped giggling.

It grew quiet.

And then Oliver said, "I don't feel like talking."

"Okay," Carol said, "okay. I have no idea what exactly is going on, but we're trying to run a children's camp here. And so we have a choice. Either we let this derail us or we take a deep breath and pick up where we left off. It's up to you. I just want to have it on the record that I prefer the latter."

Again it was quiet.

"You have no idea what's going on?" Tycho asked.

Carol sighed. "Okay, that's not entirely true. But to be honest, I don't care what people do in the privacy of their bedrooms. And personally I believe none of us should be worrying about that." She looked pointedly at Sherilynn.

"The only thing that's important right now is our Little World. So come on, let's not waste any more time talking about it, and let's leave this kitchen as a team— Carol and her Four Fantastic Juniors. Whaddaya say?"

For a moment the room was quiet. It was a slightly

less chilly silence than before, but it still had sharp edges. Then Oliver shrugged his shoulders. Tycho nodded. Donna nodded too, and Sherilynn said, "Sure, fine by me."

"Good," Carol said. "Thank you. Then we'll leave it at that. Go off and enjoy yourselves, and I'll see you when the kids get back."

They walked off. Donna let out a relieved laugh and said she was going to take the longest and hottest shower of her entire life. Oliver and Tycho headed for their supply closet. Sherilynn walked a few feet ahead of them, alone.

TYCHO WAS STRETCHED OUT on the bed. Oliver was sitting next to him, trying to untangle the string of his sweatpants. It was as if everything in the room—their unzipped bags, toothbrushes, clothes, the alarm clock, the shelves, the loom, the shoes they'd kicked off onto the floor—was trying to be very normal. Nothing going on, nothing at all. Tycho felt reassured. These objects weren't making an issue out of anything.

A knock on the door. A voice: "Can we come in?" Brahim.

"Of course!" Tycho called out. Brahim entered with Adele and Josine in tow.

"Wow, it's tiny in here," Adele said. They looked

around for somewhere to sit. On a pillow on the floor, their backs against the locker and the door.

"We just wanted to come say hi," Josine began, and laughed at herself.

"Sorry," she said, "that's a dumb way to start. We want you guys to know that if it's true what John told us at the meeting . . ."

"What did he tell you?" Oliver asked.

"Um . . . He basically said that you guys are together now. But we just wanted to let you know that we don't have a problem with that. We don't mind at all. We've come to congratulate you." Josine, Adele, Brahim—all three of them looked from Oliver to Tycho.

Oliver didn't say anything.

Tycho felt the warmth of their smiles seeping into his body. He said, "Thank you" and asked what else Director John had said. He was surprised that the camp director had told them the truth. See? he thought. Things aren't so bad. He smiled and was about to ask another question, but then he glanced over at Oliver. Oliver wasn't saying anything. Immediately Tycho thought: Oh, then I better keep quiet too.

Josine got up and said, "I think the kids are due back any minute. We have to go outside." Brahim and Adele fluffed the pillows and handed them to Tycho. They smiled and Tycho smiled back, but not too broadly. He watched them go, closed the door behind them, and turned back to Oliver. Oliver got up and said, "Right, we should go too."

THE CEO OF KNOXVILLE Little World, whose pool and whose barbecue they'd become familiar with earlier, had hosted two children and was now staying the night at the camp to get a taste of the atmosphere. And to catch up with Director John—old friends, jokes, loud voices. He came up to Tycho and asked, "How's it going?"

Tycho was about to say "Fine," but just in time he thought: Careful now.

"Could be better," he said.

"Is something wrong?" the CEO asked, scanning the room. He saw Director John gesturing toward the soda machine. Before Tycho could explain, the CEO asked, "Have you talked to John about it?"

"Yeah," he began, but before he was able to add a "but" the CEO said, "Good! I'm sure he'll be able to help you." He patted Tycho on the shoulder and walked away.

"These silly rules!" he shouted over at the camp director. "Why don't we have any beer here?"

TYCHO FELT EMPTY. DRAINED. He wanted to leave—he was ready to go to bed.

"I'm beat."

Oliver went with him.

They trudged side by side down the long hallway, past all the pictures of girls and boys the school was proud of, the showers on the left and the staff room on the right, then around the corner, to the dorm with twenty sleeping children inside it. Into their supply closet—thankfully, Oliver didn't feel like talking anymore either and, thankfully, Oliver crawled into his bed rather than climbing up into his own bunk.

There they were, snuggled up. Tycho's eyes closed. He no longer heard anything. Not Oliver's uneven breathing. Not Oliver mumbling something into his hair, whispering something: "I don't want to stay here anymore . . ."

Stay where?

Tycho didn't ask.

He slept.

NOT FOR LONG. OLIVER yanked back the covers. "I don't want to stay here anymore. Come with me."

What was happening? What was he doing? He got out of bed and fumbled for his clothes. Was he leaving? Don't hesitate, Tycho thought, go with him. He got up too. Shoes, socks, T-shirt.

"Oliver! Where are you going?"

"Outside!"

He was already at the door.

"No! Wait!" Tycho grabbed what was within reach: his wallet, the unused sleeping bag. Oliver turned the door handle, took a quick peek into the dorm, and strode off, down the aisle between the beds. Tycho followed him.

There was an eerie silence in the hallways, and Oliver was walking quickly. He went into the leaders' room, turned the light on, and went over to a list that hung on the wall. PROPERTY REGULATIONS, it said. He scanned the text and tapped his finger against the paper. Then he grabbed the key to the front door off a shelf. Lights out, and on they went. Through the auditorium, key in the lock, push, push, push, and there they were—outside, in the still-warm summer night air. They paused for a moment.

"Where are we going?"

Oliver abruptly turned his head and looked at Tycho.

"No idea."

THE SCHOOL GROUNDS WERE lit up by floodlights. Oliver avoided them. He'd started walking again. Down the driveway, toward the high fence with the barbed wire. The gate was closed. He was panting. But after a while he slowed down and even offered to carry the sleeping bag. He stopped prowling along the perimeter of the fence and turned back to Tycho. His eyes were brighter now. "Let's get out of here," he said. "I've had enough of the camp. We've got better things to do."

"Do you really want to leave?" Tycho asked.

"Yes. With you."

A tidal wave of heat flooded Tycho's body. "Me too." He put out his hand and stroked Oliver's arm.

"I'm not going back in there," Oliver said.

"You don't have to. Why don't we sleep out here?" Tycho laughed.

He was still holding his wallet. He looked at it.

Oliver started to laugh too. Just for a moment, and then he stopped abruptly, as if it hurt.

"I'm sorry," he said, "but I really want to leave. And I'll find a way."

Tycho took a step toward him, and, at exactly the same moment, they lifted their hands to each other's faces.

"Let's sleep underneath the stars," Tycho said, "and then tomorrow we'll figure out what to do. We're together—that's all that matters."

"Yeah," Oliver said, "okay. Where should we lie down?"

"I know a great spot," Tycho said, "come on."

THE TWO OF THEM could have fit inside one sleeping bag, but Tycho ran back inside to get another, and their pillows. When he got back Oliver was sitting on the ground waiting, his elbows on his knees, staring off into the night.

"We'll have a perfect view from up here tomorrow morning," Tycho said. He zipped the two sleeping bags together and started making their bed on the luke-warm concrete.

"Mm," Oliver said.

Tycho had dragged him to the little stadium, half-way down the track and then up into the bleachers. They'd climbed up all the way to the top, where they had a view of the fences and the road, with the school behind them.

Tycho said, "What do you think?" and Oliver duti-fully took off his shoes, put his socks and his sweat-pants next to the bed, and slid into the sleeping bag. "Goodnight," he sighed—apparently, he wasn't in the mood for "welterusten"—and he turned around, put his head on Tycho's shoulder, and fell asleep.

IT WAS A BLOTCHY sort of night. The heat still hung in the air and mixed unevenly with the creep-ing cold. The sky was stretched over the city like a pale cowskin. A few stars here and there, scattered glitter stuck in someone's hair.

Now Tycho lay awake. He'd folded his arms to make a second pillow and could feel Oliver's breath, now calm and regular, against his left ear.

How quickly things can change, he thought. Two hours ago we were still lying in there, in a room without windows with a sky of mattress. And now open sky is all there is. Quite a backdrop. Quite a movie. Not bad, he thought, not bad.

A little later still, he thought: We're halfway. Tomorrow we're leaving. Oliver is leading the way, I'll fly behind him. *Take a journey, take a walk.*

N o," OLIVER SAID.
Tycho jolted awake, half-sitting up. Oof, that sun! And why was he wet? His sleeping bag and his T-shirt were clammy. What from? Dew? He opened his eyes a little further. Boots. Shit! A police officer's boots! And Oliver, standing beside the sleeping bag.

Two cops, asking who they were. Why they were lying here. Didn't they know minors weren't allowed to be in public places at this hour? Oh, they were from Europe? Then why were they here? They weren't underage? Were they able to prove that? What kind of camp? Carol? Carol who?

"You two stay here," the police officers said. They didn't even sound that unfriendly. They headed for the school building and Oliver looked over at Tycho.

"Good morning!" he said.

Tycho said, "Trouble?"

"Nah," Oliver said.

Tycho got dressed and started rolling up the sleeping bag. "No?" he said.

"We'll see how it goes," Oliver said. "Who knows."

Tycho looked at him. He said, "Okay. Who knows." But the shoelaces he was tying trembled, along with his fingers.

F ROM THAT MOMENT ON, things happened so fast it almost felt unreal. Afterwards Tycho would only be able to recall the beginning, a moment from the middle, and the finale.

The beginning: Carol—still in her nightie and slippers—making her way toward them with the two police officers, standing on the track and holding up their passports so they could see that Tycho and Oliver were real and were both over eighteen. Director John following behind in a bathrobe and with bed hair. The cops saying, "Thank you, you take care now." The director not looking at them and stomping back to the school. Carol shaking her head and sighing, "Boys, you're really in trouble now . . ."

A bit from the middle: the kids sitting up in bed, awake, wide-eyed, watching as Oliver and Tycho brought the sleeping bags back inside. The camp director coming to get them, the CEO following close behind.

And the end: the full staff room, Carol, Gary, the camp director, and the CEO. The CEO, whom they saw through the little window, shaking his head, and Carol gesturing, and the camp director calling them in and launching into a speech that ended with the words, "I'm sorry, but I have no choice. One of the rules at all of the Little World camps is that anyone who comes into contact with the police in any way is excluded from . . ."

"But," Tycho said, "we didn't—"

"Quiet," Oliver said.

". . . further participation. I'm really so sorry."

D IRECTOR JOHN TOOK A deep breath, sighed, took another deep breath, and said, "I'm sending you home."

Halftime

JUST ONE LITTLE NUDGE and it all smashed apart. So quickly, so suddenly. To such dazzling effect.

Tycho loved this violence, the unpredictable rolling around that sent one running off to the left and the other to the right. He liked the strange forces at work. Everything was responding to a law—a law that always played out differently than it had the time before, differently than it would the next time. A law that kept you on your toes.

Oliver and Tycho stood on either side of a pool table and nodded at each other. Another round? Wanna go again? Tycho watched Oliver arrange the balls in the rack, pushing and sliding until they were in the right place. He watched him very carefully lift the rack off the table, appraising the triangle of balls in the middle of the green. He watched him wrap his fingers around a cue, slowly walk over to the table, and take aim. He hesitated once or twice, took a few feints, and then, all of a sudden: a quick jab against the white ball, a clack, a crash, and the triangle exploded in a starburst of colors. Tycho watched the balls scatter toward the corners of the table and come to a halt—how beautiful, this new order that had emerged, everything shaken up and rearranged. Oliver grinned.

Now what? Tycho thought. Now what?

Now began the puzzle—the task of dissecting the chaos and getting the balls home again one by one, all in the right order, into their designated pockets at the edges of the table.

Tycho never knew where to begin, but Oliver's eyes were twinkling. He said, "I like this."

D ELTA 2728. KLM 622. Director John had already booked their return flights. They'd be flying from Knoxville to Atlanta that same night, and travel on from there the next morning. Even Carol, who took them to the kitchen for tea and a quick breakfast, made it clear there was no point in protesting. "It's the rules," she said. "All I can say is I didn't make them."

She took them back to their supply closet. They walked past the staff room, where Brahim was gesturing and they could hear Josine's voice, loud and angry, and past the boys' dorm, empty now, and they thought: Where is everyone? Carol said, "The flagpole"—*all of us can feel at ease, spread the joy and spread the peace.*

They had to pack and Carol helped them, folding clothes and tucking dirty socks into side pockets, quick and neat, with the hands of a mother and the eyes of a frustrated manager—not quite high up enough on the ladder to make a difference.

Josine came in with Brahim. They said, "Oof, you guys . . ." and "Don't let it get to you," kind words meant to help them past their anger. They hugged Tycho, they hugged Oliver, and didn't look at Carol. Paddy One and Paddy Two came running in—"Hey hey hey!"—followed by Adele. More hugs.

Gary showed up. Time to go. It turned out there was a back exit where the CEO's car was already waiting. Gary held out his hand, but they both refused to shake it.

"Aw, guys . . ." Gary said.

Carol got a kiss on the cheek. "Hang in there," Brahim repeated. Josine: "See you." Adele: "All the best." Oliver and Tycho gave each of the Paddys a gentle punch on the arm.

D ONNA!" SUDDENLY TYCHO REMEMBERED Donna.

"Donna's not feeling well," Gary said.

"Oh? Where is she?" Tycho asked.

"She's asleep," Gary said.

"Can we still go see her?" Tycho asked.

"I don't think that's such a good idea," Gary said. The CEO opened the car doors. He'd put their suitcases in the trunk.

"Okay, who's going in front?"

"We're both going in the back," Oliver said.

They climbed in and as the engine started, they heard Donna shouting "Tycho! Tycho!" She didn't sound sick or sleepy. She ran over to the car and started banging her hands on the windshield. Carol grabbed her. Tycho got out, and Donna flung herself into his arms. He didn't know what to do. Donna was sobbing, and he patted her back awkwardly. The CEO impatiently revved the engine.

"It's okay," Tycho said, "it's okay, Donna." He had stopped rubbing her back, and Carol gently pried Donna's arms off him. Donna let her. Tycho leaned over and quickly whispered something into her ear. She looked up and Tycho saw her expression change as she took in his words.

"Bye," Tycho said, "bye."

He got back into the car. The doors slammed shut. They waved. The Paddys ran alongside for a bit. The others stood still. Where was the camp director?

The car slowly glided around the corner and out through the gate.

THE BASEMENT HAD A bathroom, a pool table, a pinball machine, a stereo, a home cinema, a sectional. They were allowed to use the pool, though they couldn't remember where they'd put their swimming trunks. Every now and then the CEO's wife poked her head downstairs to ask if they wanted anything to eat or drink.

Tycho knew he was being scrutinized, perceived as a strange phenomenon, but somehow he didn't mind. He'd whispered it into Donna's ear himself: "We want to leave. We want to leave together." All the events of the past twenty-four hours had done was lead the way. A storm? Yes, but one blowing at their back.

Oliver cheered as he potted two balls. Tycho had asked him how he felt about the camp director, and he'd said, "John? He's the manager, that's just how it is."

"What about us?" Tycho had asked.

"We're the players," Oliver had said.

You're the one I want to be with, Tycho had thought. For longer than just the flight home.

ONE MORE DAY, TYCHO thought, the Delta 2728, the KLM 622—and then what?

"Where should we go?" Tycho asked. "My parents won't be home for another week and your mother will be gone all month."

Oliver relaxed his aim and stood upright. He looked at Tycho, put his cue down, and flopped onto the sofa. He dropped his arms to his sides and said, "Yeah, so?"

"Well," Tycho said hesitantly, "we'll both come home to an empty house."

"Yeah . . ." Oliver said. He nodded. "So?"

"I just wanted to know," Tycho said, "where you want to go."

Oliver got up and walked back to the pool table.

Suddenly, he grabbed his cue and brandished it like a sword. He shouted, "We wanted to go home and now we're *going* home! Don't worry!" He walked toward Tycho, jabbing at the air, once, twice, three times.

"But which home?" Tycho said. He grabbed a cue too, threw it into the air with his right hand, caught it in his left, and threw it again, like a swordfighter showing off his ambidextrous moves. He hunched his shoulders when he saw Oliver doing the same and— *thwack!*—he mock-thrust it at his friend, the two cues knocking against each other.

Oliver parried the blow and then lunged at Tycho's stomach, but Tycho blocked him. Left, right, left, right, legs apart, knees bent, one foot in front of the other, your free hand held up in the air, ready to show mercy to your opponent—or not—when they fell to the ground. But it didn't come to that, because Oliver grabbed Tycho's cue and pulled it out of his hands.

"Hey, that's not fair!" Tycho shouted, but a Norwegian-style hip throw had already landed him back on the sofa. Oliver straddled him: "Tell me," he said, "tell me what you want."

"I want 'da da da so what,'" Tycho said, laughing.

His voice had dropped to the back of his throat and everything was tickly.

"That's right!" Oliver said, and Tycho became aware of how close he was and how they were lying there, sitting there. He pulled his captor toward him, and suddenly they found themselves in the heat of another kind of battle.

THE ROOM WAS A soap bubble. Any moment something from the outside could burst it, and to get out ahead of that they needed to get hotter and heavier than they had at the camp. They whipped off their T-shirts and pulled all the other fabric out of the way with impatient fingers. They pushed against each other, switching gears in an instant, from second to sixth to eleventh to twenty-eighth. It was as if there was something to be triumphed over, something big surrounding them that melted away when they made each other spark. Champions League sex, Tycho thought halfway through. He whispered it out loud: "Champions League sex." He'd never said those words before, but for some reason they made him feel strong and powerful.

And when it was over and they'd both caught their breath and wiped themselves clean, when they were all dry and dressed again and were taking stock of the situation, they felt like they'd just completed a half marathon. If anything had been bothering them over the last few hours, days, weeks, they'd driven it howling back into the forest. The camp was a closed chapter. It was just the two of them now, and they were flying together. And then what?

"Oliver," Tycho said, pressing his head into the back of the sofa, "don't you think it's time you asked me if I want to come back home with you?"

And Oliver asked quietly, "Do you want to come back home with me?"

Tycho nodded.

A little later the CEO's wife came in, with lunch and without knocking. The bubble burst, and Oliver and Tycho cracked up laughing.

THEN THE WAITING BEGAN. They waited in the car to the airport, while they crawled around the parking garage, in front of a counter, at the back of the check-in line. The CEO shook their hands and gave them their tickets and an envelope. They strolled off, following the signs, past all the shops, where they bought candy and Coke.

The envelope was from Director John. "What?" Tycho said. "Huh? This is a printout of an email. That asshole went and emailed my parents!"

Oliver laughed. "Give me that," he said, pulling the piece of paper out of Tycho's hands. He folded it open, quickly scanned it, and then tore it in half. Again, and again.

Tycho looked at him. "Now what?"

"Now nothing," Oliver said. He gave the torn-up bits of paper back to Tycho. He could still make out the words "sorry," "homosexuality," and "parents." Tycho crumpled the shreds, balled them up in his hand, and threw them into a trash can.

THEY WERE LYING ON a bench at their gate. Again they were waiting. Oliver was sprawled out, reading a book that he held over his face like a tent. His knees were hooked over the armrest and his feet dangled above the floor.

Tycho had curled up next to him. He was thinking. He couldn't get the word "parents" from the letter out of his mind. So Director John was trying to inform his parents. The question was whether he was going to succeed at that. They were in Southampton—no, he was going to have to tell them himself. But calling them now would cost a fortune. Maybe he could do it in Norway. Truthfully, he didn't want to have to explain Oliver, the truth, himself, or his decision to go to Gjøvik over the phone. He could just send the message he'd drafted before, but that would only raise questions. Or he could email them himself. Yes, that's what he should do. Write an honest email to his parents, one that would make John's pale by comparison.

There was an internet terminal at the gate. He explained his plan to Oliver, who listened and nodded. Tycho sat down at one of the computers and took a deep breath.

I T ENDED UP BEING a pretty long message. He tried to be as persuasive as possible, even though he wasn't sure his parents were checking their emails regularly. Did they even know where to find an internet shop in Southampton? His parents needed to know that this was what he wanted, that what the camp director had written didn't matter, that he was happy and more himself than he'd ever been. That they would have a proper talk once they were all back home. That he hoped they understood him. That he was coming home in two weeks' time, as planned, just from a different country. That he loved them. Yes, he wasn't afraid to write that. And just as Oliver came over to say it was time to board, Tycho hit send.

A FTER THE JOURNEY, WHICH seemed to take longer than the flight out, Tycho hurried to the transfer desk at Schiphol Airport. Yes, you could buy tickets here. No, there were no seats left on the morning flight, and yes, there was still one available on a departure three hours later. Tycho ran over to an ATM. He spent the rest of his plum-thinning wages on a ticket to Oslo—date of return flight still to be determined—valid for one month. He weighed the piece of paper in his hand, looking at the red letters:

ZELING, T MR.

He felt confident and decisive—like someone leaping from the roof of one train to another, from the bed of one truck to another, from one two-week period into another.

He ran back to Oliver. "I've got a ticket!" he shouted. "They still had seats!"

"Yeah, of course," Oliver said. "Who would want to go to Norway?"

THE PLAN WAS FOR Oliver to wait for Tycho to land at the airport just outside Oslo, sometime around 7:00 p.m., and then they'd take the train to Gjøvik together.

Tycho felt like jumping for joy. He ran over to a café and bought two paninis, which they quickly wolfed down. When Oliver had to go, Tycho squeezed his hand to a pulp. And when he said "See you later, right?" one more time, he gave him a kiss—which made Oliver frown and the flight attendant smile.

He walked along the windows to wave and looked up into the blue sky to follow Oliver, squinting into the bright light. Then he ran into a restroom and shouted "Thank you!" at the fly in the urinal.

Second Half

"HEY," OLIVER SAID, "WE have to hurry." He grabbed Tycho's suitcase and put it on a trolley. He was smiling, but at the same time, he started pushing the cart away. Tycho ran after him—"Wait! Not so fast!"—and let his eyes wander around the terminal to get his bearings. Signs and counters and colors and racks full of magazines outside the newsstand. Two crying children, a tour guide holding up a sign (STAVANGER TOURS), Oliver's back, his feet and his coat flapping as he walked. Oliver gestured for him to hurry up. Down an escalator, onto a bus. Oliver showed their tickets to the driver, who glanced pointedly at his watch. Tycho lifted the suitcases into a rack and stumbled after Oliver, who chose a two-seater. They slid into their seats and the doors closed. Tycho tried to think of something to say to Oliver, something that would make him happy, but Oliver pointed at the screens that hung down throughout the bus. They flashed on, and a lady appeared, smiling, talking, and walking into a brown building.

"That's where we're going," Oliver said, "to Oslo train station. And then on to Gjøvik."

Tycho looked at him. Oliver gestured for him to pay attention to the screen.

Of course, Tycho thought. He just wants to go home. He's been sitting around for hours waiting for me. On a bench, with all of his stuff. No wonder he's in a hurry.

"Are you tired?" he asked.

"I'm okay," Oliver said.

He was looking out the window now. So was Tycho.

Cars, trees, and concrete. Billboards, overpasses. He forced himself to think. I'm in Norway, I'm with Oliver, and soon we'll be together in his house.

TYCHO SAT IN THE living room with his arms spread across the back of the sofa. He was comfortable here in this corner, his arms wide, as if he was trying to hug his new surroundings. Oliver had gone to buy food—the convenience store was still open. Tycho had said he was happy to come along, but Oliver shook his head and left.

There was a wide fireplace set into the wall straight across from him, flanked by high candlesticks—too many to count at a glance—with all sorts of candles, fat ones, short ones, thin ones, long ones, blue and white. In the middle of the room was a rug, a dark blue sea stretched across the floorboards. Not many plants.

The rear window looked out onto mountains. Well,

compared to the mountains in America these were hills, really, but still . . . Their walk here from the little train station had already been a climb. The moon was full, the sky was cloudless, and he saw little lights in the distance—houses scattered across the hillside, as if they'd been flung onto it from down below.

He got up and walked across the room. Here at the front of the house, you looked out onto nothing. Farmland. A streetlight. Part of the porch. No neighbors across the street.

In the open-plan kitchen he saw Oliver in his mother's arms in a picture tacked to a corkboard. The picture had been taken in a garden, and Oliver was small and smiling, half-genuinely. His mother was holding on to him as if she was determined to never let him go. There were other pictures too. Oliver's football team. Strange people, relatives maybe. A kitten. But Tycho's gaze kept drifting back to the one with Oliver's mother.

"Hi, Oliver's mom," he said. "I'm Tycho."

Stina was her name; he already knew that from Oliver. And that's what it said on the nameplate by the front door: STINA SOLHEIM, OLIVER KJELSBERG. Both of their names in full, like he was the man of the house. Which he was, in a way, but you couldn't tell from the nameplate that she was the mother and he was the son. His father lived somewhere up north. Oliver went to visit him sometimes. You could ski there, he'd said. He didn't see him very often. Good, Tycho had thought, that means I don't have to meet him.

And his mother? He'd worry about that later.

"Sorry, Stina," he said, "but for now I'm secretly living with your son."

She didn't bat an eyelid, but clasped her little boy close.

It put Tycho in a good mood. Maybe he should light the candles? Put on some music? Make coffee? After just an hour in this house, was it okay for him to go rummaging through the kitchen cabinets in search of coffee filters?

Yes, he decided. He looked around the room and thought: Ultimately, this is the stadium where Oliver and I will be playing the second half of our match. This room, Gjøvik, Norway. He chuckled. It was a flawed analogy, of course—he and Oliver had shaken off their opponent, so it wasn't going to be a real match. What then? An after-party?

OLIVER CAME HOME. FROM the kitchen window Tycho saw him riding his bike into the shed. Tycho waved. Oliver held something up in the air. A bag. After some clumping around by the back door, wiping, stomping, he came into the living room.

"I've got it," he said. He took his coat off and pulled

two flat boxes from the bag. "Peppe's Pizza, Gjøvik's best."

Tycho said, "We're not going to cook?"

"Not tonight. I'm not that great at it anyway, my mother does it most of the time."

"Now you tell me," Tycho said. "I guess that means I'm stuck with the job."

"That's just fine by me," Oliver said and gave him a whack on the shoulder.

Tycho laughed. Okay then. He wasn't going to be able to just sit on his ass.

"Time to pop in a video," Oliver continued, from the other side of the bar that separated the kitchen and the living room.

"A movie?" Tycho said.

"Yeah. To help with the jet lag. We can't go to bed just yet," Oliver said, grinning.

Pizza. Coke. Five inches of space on the sofa between their sprawled bodies. Their feet were up on a little table, their toes pointing into the air. Oliver had drawn the curtains and lit the candles. Keanu Reeves and River Phoenix played the leads in the movie. There was a scene by a campfire where Keanu and River talked at cross-purposes about the difference between friendship and love.

Every time they sat back after leaning over to put

down a plate or grab a glass, Oliver and Tycho moved closer together. Minus four, three, two inches—until they were snuggled up together, watching the two friends on the screen. Fortunately, their own romance didn't entirely mirror the one in the movie, which took a tragic turn. River went to pieces. By the end he had lost everything and just lay there, sick and totally alone, as the credits washed over him.

They loved the movie. There was not an inch left between Oliver and Tycho, and they were full of River. "Then it hits you that he's dead . . ." Oliver said. "An overdose, at twenty-three."

Tycho sighed. Beautiful. And sad. Strange, this ending to a long day. A day of oceans and hills and sky.

"Let's go to bed," Oliver said. He blew out the candles. "Come on."

He led Tycho down the hallway, holding his hands out behind his back. Tycho slipped his hands into Oliver's and followed along behind him into one of the rooms. They undressed, yawning, threw their clothes onto the floor, cuddled up, and almost immediately sank into a deep, deep sleep.

A SHAFT OF MORNING LIGHT fell onto Tycho's face, as if the Norwegian sun had become aware of this new visitor and wanted to get a better look at him. It woke him up. He shifted slightly to get out of its glare. He blinked, and, once his eyes had gotten used to the light, looked around the room.

Oliver must have gotten up—his clothes were no longer on the floor. In the middle of the wall across from the bed stood a bare, tidy desk: a globe, a computer, a stack of books with the big ones at the bottom and the small ones on top. Above the desk, a pinboard full of pennants, ribbons, and medals, and a shelf with trophies and cups, all lined up from big to small. The Norway Cup.

Old football shoes hung from a nail on the wall. Next to them was a row of posters of different teams— Barcelona, Swansea, Gjøvik FF, Rosenborg, Ajax—and next to the window, a gallery of Oliver's favorite players. Tycho read their names. David Beckham, Steffen Iversen, Bjørn Tore Kvarme, Michael Owen, and the only one Tycho knew: Frank de Boer.

The Norway Cup? Tycho thought. Hadn't Oliver mentioned that before? Suddenly he felt a little guilty. He was just lying here when Oliver was probably busy making breakfast or tidying up.

He got up, then bent over and gathered his clothes. There was a sock behind the door. Tycho pushed and the door slammed shut. He started hopping around on one foot when his toes got stuck in the sock, but then out of the corner of his eye he saw blotches, skin tones. He looked up. On the door there was a life-size poster of a guy he knew—hair half-obscuring his eyes, a guarded gaze, a beautiful nose, a shy mouth, and a white chest with black letters: RIVER PHOENIX. Tycho stood up straight, despite his sock, which was still all tangled up and caught on his toenails.

O LIVER WAS SQUEEZING ORANGES. The kitchen table was all set. Tycho felt his body start to glow. The kitchen, the table, the orange juice, and the look on Oliver's face—all of it seemed like an invitation: come on in, take a seat.

"Hi," Oliver said. "Sleep well?"

"Yeah," Tycho said. "You?"

"Yeah, me too. Did you see my mom?" Oliver poured two tumblers full of juice and put them in the top left corners of the two place mats, exactly in line with each other. He nodded his head toward the photo on the pinboard.

"Yeah," Tycho said. "She seems nice."

"She is," Oliver said.

"Where exactly is she again?"

"Um . . . Tanzania, I think. And then Kenya after that."

"That must be interesting."

"Yeah."

"Do you talk to her often?"

"How do you mean? Of course."

"You know, about football and stuff . . ."

"Sure, why wouldn't I?"

"And about that River Phoenix poster?"

"What about it?"

"Does she know you like him?"

"Of course she does. We watch his movies together."

"And what about your friends? What do they say when they see your room?"

"My friends don't come up to my room."

"I do."

"Yeah, but you're different."

Tycho smiled. Oliver sliced some bread. One slice, and then another. Another, and another. Lots of bread.

"Do you think your mother's okay with me being here?"

Oliver looked up.

"Of course. She won't mind at all."

It was still sunny. Stina was smiling in the picture. It was still morning too. But on the kitchen table, crumbs, spilled salt, knives, forks, empty glasses, and creases in the tablecloth had turned order into chaos.

OLIVER PREFERRED TO STAY at home all the time. "You know," he said, "just the two of us." Tycho was fine with that. I'll follow his lead, Tycho thought, we're in his hometown, in his country. The walls of his Norwegian home kept the outside world at bay. Oliver had put away his cellphone, or turned it off—Tycho hadn't seen him with it since they'd arrived. He for his part had dashed off a vague message to Southampton, since his parents had asked if things were going well. *All good*, he'd typed, *having fun, more later.* So they hadn't read the camp director's email, or his own. Good. He put his cellphone away. Clearly Oliver wanted to block out everything and everyone to be with him, and Tycho wanted exactly the same thing.

Oliver had bought groceries based on Tycho's instructions. Tycho had offered to come along again, but Oliver shook his head. "You're the guest," he said. In any case, they now had enough vegetables, chicken, and rice to last them at least seven days. Sometimes Oliver would even draw the curtains. Tycho admired his boyfriend's pragmatic attitude: they were here—right now now now, for who knew how much longer—so they had to make every second count.

O F ALL THE ROOMS in the house, the bathroom was the perfect hideaway. No windows, locks on the door, thick, fluffy towels, and steam and hot water. The two of them fit in the tub together, their arms hanging over the edge. They grinned at each other stupidly and blew handfuls of bubbles back and forth, until one of them leaned in for soap or a kiss or started splashing the other with water maybe and they had to tussle and have sex. And that didn't stop until the water really was too cold.

ONCE, THE DOORBELL RANG. They were sitting on the floor in the living room and playing Trivial Pursuit, the Norwegian version. Tycho read out the questions and Oliver translated them. Tycho pretended he was determined to catch up with Oliver, who was ahead, while Oliver pretended he was determined to avoid that at all costs. They drank hot chocolate and every now and then rubbed their socked feet together.

Until the doorbell rang.

"Shit!" Oliver said and jumped up. He motioned for Tycho to lie still and shimmied over to the window with his back to the wall. He leaned over, almost pressing his nose against the glass, and sighed, "Oh! Just the postman." He ran to front door and opened it. Moments later, he came back into the living room and said, "Registered mail from America."

Oliver hadn't given them an email, but apparently, the camp management did have his home address.

He tore the envelope open and began reading. "Dear Mr. and Mrs. Kjelsberg." He paused and looked up. "Well, they got that part wrong."

He read on. "It's the same letter they gave you. 'Disciplinary reasons,' yada yada."

"Wow, they won't let it go, will they," Tycho said.

"Yeah . . . Gotta go by the book," Oliver said. He crumpled the piece of paper into a ball and threw it into the kitchen. Then he got up. "John," he said, "The camp dick. Want more to drink?"

THE DAYS WERE LOVELY. It was sunny all the time and yet it didn't get hot. They wore T-shirts and shorts but there was enough of a breeze that they weren't dripping with sweat all day. They spent as much time in the backyard as they did in the house. They played games and had sex for as long as they lasted—it made Tycho dizzy sometimes. The hours on the clock went uncounted, blurring into long, leisurely days.

Even better were the evenings, when Tycho would watch from the side window of the kitchen as Oliver lit the storm lantern on the patio table for later, when dusk fell. Tycho chopped vegetables, diced chicken breasts, and made pans sizzle with olive oil. He eased sauce onto plates, tasted with a teaspoon, and fluffed steamed rice. He was good at this. He'd been doing this every weekend since he was about four years old. Back home that was just normal, but here—here it was "wow!" and "unbelievable!" when Oliver came up behind him, peered over his shoulder, and wrapped his fingers around his hips.

On one of these nights, long after dinner, they were sitting staring up at the sky above the hill, watching the first stars appear. They were drinking Munkholm beer and talking. Talking about fathers.

"I don't miss him," Oliver said. "Whenever he sees me he feels guilty. When he doesn't see me, he forgets all about me. That's why I make sure he keeps seeing me from time to time."

Talking about the camp. "So why did you want to leave?" Tycho asked.

Oliver thought for a moment. "I wanted freedom, I think. Didn't you want that too?"

"I'm glad we didn't stay," Tycho said. "Hey, did you know we weren't supposed to be out at night?"

Oliver laughed. "Sort of?"

"Did you do that on purpose?"

"Sort of. Didn't you know that?"

"Maybe," Tycho said, "sort of." Something flashed through his mind. An arrow that hit its target, landing somewhere that worried him. He shook his head. The night was still balmy. One by one the lights of the houses on the hillside across from them were going out. Tycho cast about for a different topic. "What is there to do around here?"

"Nothing. Gjøvik is dead. Staying in is more exciting."

"But shouldn't I see a bit of this country?"

"Hmm. I'll think about it." An owl hooted in the distance.

"You know what I spent ages hoping for?" Oliver said after a minute. "That I'd be scouted. As a football pro. But I'm almost too old now."

Tycho gave Oliver a sidelong glance and Oliver looked back. He tucked his hair behind his ears, leaned over, blew out the tea light in the storm lantern, and lifted one foot onto the sofa, sliding it behind Tycho's back. Tycho pulled his legs up to his chest and crawled into the V his boyfriend had made for him. There he was, sprawled between Oliver's muscular thighs—until he felt an exclamation mark pulsing against the small of his back. He turned around, and moments later they both got up and hurriedly stumbled to Oliver's too-narrow bed.

L ATER, A LITTLE LATER, during the night, when Tycho was rummaging through his suitcase for tissues, he saw his cellphone again. Suddenly he grew curious. The battery was dead, so he grabbed his charger, went to the kitchen, plugged it in, and checked his messages. There were just a few. Mainly from his parents, of course. Nothing unusual—they were still asking how things were going, they were still telling him about the rainy weather in the south of England. Tycho wrote back: *Love from over here, everything is fine, and hectic, and fun.* He walked back to the bedroom, threw his phone into his suitcase, onto his clothes, and slid back into bed.

Oliver clicked the bedside light on. "Any news?" he asked.

"Nothing important," Tycho said.

"Your parents?" Oliver asked. "Or John?"

"Parents." Tycho laughed. "Don't worry, John's done with us. Go back to sleep."

Oliver sat up. "You know what," he said. "I feel like writing him a postcard. An old-fashioned postcard that would get there on the last day of camp."

"Why? What would you want to write?"

"Something polite," Oliver said. "Something grateful."

Tycho chuckled. "Sure, why not. 'You're the best camp director we know.'"

"How many camp directors do we know?"

"Just the one."

"Okay, so you just want to write something nice?"

"No. He needs to know that we're here together."

"Thanks to him."

"Dear John, thank you so much."

"Love to Gary."

"And the CEO."

"And his wife."

"And his swimming pool."

"And his pool table."

"And his balls."

They lay back down. "Lots of love from Norway," Tycho said. "How should we write our names?"

"Just our initials," Oliver said, "but not in ink."

"No?"

"No. Something else," Oliver said, reaching down toward Tycho's briefs.

I T'S SO QUIET, TYCHO thought on the third morning. Oliver had gone to get fresh milk and a loaf of bread. He'd said so in a note he left on the door, with a second note underneath it that said, BE RIGHT BACK. Tycho was standing barefoot in the backyard, listening. He heard birdsong, but nothing else—no children, no cars. In America there'd been noise, constant noise. And constant action.

Here it was quiet. Here he and Oliver spent all day staring at each other. Tycho sat down on the patio sofa. He pictured Oliver in motion. Reaching up to get mugs from one of the kitchen cabinets, turning the pages of a book, getting chairs out of the shed, pointing out the ski-jumping hill in the distance from the backyard, and the school, the gymnasium, and the football pitches; how he'd gone and fetched his trophies from his room one by one and told Tycho about each of them and pointed himself out on the Gjøvik FF poster. Two and a half weeks ago all of that had been new to Tycho, and now he could conjure up Oliver's movements in his head, just like that. He smiled. For a moment he'd thought he might be homesick for the US—but no, that was ridiculous. There was still so much for him to discover here: the streets of this town, the stores, the pool, Oliver's school, maybe his football friends . . .

He drummed his hands on the armrest of the sofa. He got up and shook out his feet. He jumped into the air as high as he could. He dove forward and did a few push-ups. He laughed at the mountains and whooped at the birds: "Heeeeyaaaaah!"

"Starting to go a little crazy?"

Oliver nudged the wooden gate open with the front wheel of his bike. Tycho ran up to him and shouted "Yes!" He took the plastic bag off him. The gate slammed shut. Oliver stood still. He leaned in toward Tycho for a kiss and said, "Hi." Tycho grabbed the handlebars with both hands and swung one leg over the front wheel. "Listen," he said. "I really want to get out and do something today. Where should we go?"

Oliver looked back at him. There they stood, one boy across from the other. He said, "Um, all right . . .

Maybe later? Let's chill out for now, okay?" He lowered his eyes.

Tycho let go of the handlebars.

He thought of his mother. At one point she'd come to the Netherlands from the UK. She'd seen his father and had decided to stay with him. How had that happened? Had his father taken her to meet his parents and his friends? Or had he kept her to himself for a while?

He couldn't ask them yet. He trusted that once he got home, they'd at least listen to him. They weren't a family that talked much—usually they just quietly assumed they understood each other. But when something exceptional happened—Grandpa's death, his mom going back to school, his decision to go on a trip by himself—it never took long before someone said, "Let's sit down and talk." And then the three of them ended up at the kitchen table, talking until everything had been hashed out.

Would they understand about Oliver? Would they understand why he was in Norway instead of Knoxville? He felt ashamed. Maybe he should have called them after all.

But then again, he couldn't help it if love had come crashing down onto his head. He was no hunter. Never had been. Of course, he'd met Oliver, he'd fallen in love, gone with him. But it couldn't have gone any other way. From the very first moment, he'd had no choice, as if his free will and the circumstances had all been tracks leading in the same direction.

Tycho looked through the *Aftenposten.* The *Evening Post*—that's what this paper was called. His eyes skimmed the headlines, scanning the Norwegian text for words he understood, for foreign names. Oliver came and stood next to him, looking over his shoulder. That was no good—trying to read with someone else reading along, that always drove him crazy. So he pointed at a word. "What does this say?"

"What do you think?" Oliver said, and Tycho did his best to figure out what it might mean.

It turned into a game. He guessed nine words out of twelve, but then Oliver spotted two words in the sports section that made him jump up: "Norway Cup!"

He slid the newspaper out from underneath Tycho's arms and sank down onto the floor. He read, following along with his finger. After five minutes he looked up. "There are fifteen hundred and fifty teams this year. From sixty-two different countries."

"Where?"

"In Oslo! At the Norway Cup!"

"So what exactly is this Norway Cup?"

Oliver rose to his feet and explained that the Norway Cup was the biggest youth football tournament in all of Europe. It took place just outside Oslo, on the Ekebergsletta—the Ekeberg Plain. He'd competed six times, his team played every year. They stayed in a school building, and last year they'd won everything. This year he hadn't been able to go because of Little World.

"They're leaving soon," he said. "It's supposed to be bigger than ever this time." He gestured and gestured and he grinned and ran to his room to get a photo album and show Tycho pictures. Suddenly he seemed a good few years younger.

Tycho said, "You must be bummed that you can't go this year."

It was quiet for a moment. Finally Oliver said, "Yeah. But I had to choose. So I did. And my mother wanted me to go see a bit of the world."

He folded the newspaper, put the album away, and dropped the subject.

EXCEPT FOR ONE QUESTION, a little later: "D'you know who's gonna be there too? As a guest, at the Norway Cup?"

"No?"

"Del Piero."

"Who?"

"An amazing striker, from Italy. But I guess you wouldn't know him. Never mind."

T HE SUN SHONE ONTO the backyard and Oliver
unfolded two lawn chairs. Tycho recalled being
a little kid, in elementary school. There was a field
next to the school, and as 10:30 approached, the football players in the class would start whispering themselves into teams. When the bell rang, they would all
sprint over there like a herd of deer. He usually stayed
inside playing computer games, or, when the weather
was nice, he'd go out into the bushes where he was
building a hut. Sure, from time to time he would
play too. But he was never the first to be chosen.
Sometime halfway through he'd be shoved over to one
of the teams. He'd stand there on the field like a
rock—he played defense—and sometimes, if he was
in the mood, he'd run toward everything that moved.

When he did, people would pat him on the shoulder, though no one ever said, "Good play, Tycho." No,
they'd say, "Hey, man, good effort."

Sometimes he'd watch football on TV with his
father. His father liked Heerenveen, Vitesse, NAC.
"I'm not interested in the real top," he said. "The ones
that are almost there—the fighters, the hard workers—
those are the people I respect." And then he'd slap
Tycho on the knee.

Every now and then his mother would watch too,
rating jerseys and butts. Tycho smiled. The men on
the posters in Oliver's room—they were handsome.

Suddenly he flushed hot all over. He wanted to be there when Oliver was in goal. He wanted to be the opponent's shot. He wanted Oliver to clutch him to his chest, hide him under his sweaty shirt—Tycho looked over at Oliver lying in the sun, half-asleep.

"Do you want something to drink?" he asked. He was being ridiculous—ridiculously in love. He had to do something, get something, prepare something. He got up. "A milkshake? A Coke? Ice cream?"

THE REST OF THE day, Oliver said no more about the Norway Cup. And Tycho didn't want to ask. After all, things were great, weren't they? They were having such a good time. It was as if they were living together, for real. He didn't want to rock the boat right now.

Oliver was mowing the grass. Tycho was pounding the ground beef that Oliver had bought. He was going to make burgers, onion rings, and fries with a side of corn. Maybe tomorrow they really could do something. To begin with, maybe they could climb the hill and look down at their yard from the other side of the street. *Grrr*, the lawnmower growled, *grrr*—as if it hated what it was having to do to all those poor blades of grass.

That's when the doorbell rang.

Tycho sucked in his breath. He glanced out the

window—Oliver hadn't heard anything. Should he warn him? Who could it be? The postman? With another registered letter? Or one of Oliver's friends? He slammed the meat down onto the counter and wiped his hands on the tea towel. As he was trying to slide over to the window along the wall, the doorbell rang a second time. Tycho changed tack and ran over to the door. He could still hear soft growling coming from the backyard.

"HEI," SAID THE MAN who was standing on the porch steps. He was wearing a tracksuit.

"Hello," Tycho said.

"Jeg så Oliver i byen i mom og da . . ."

"Sorry," Tycho said, "I don't understand Norwegian."

"Unnskyld meg," said the man. "Is Oliver home? I saw him on his bike this morning."

"No. He's not here."

Tycho heard himself saying the words. He finally had the chance to see a little bit of Oliver's regular life and now he was lying. Why? Because he thought Oliver would want him to? "Can I pass on a message?"

"Um . . . Yeah. I'd like him to come to Oslo with us tomorrow. I'm his football coach. I thought he was on vacation, but then I saw him on his bike this morning . . . He can still come if he wants. Tell him we need him. We're meeting at ten thirty at the football pitch. He already has the match schedule."

"Okay," Tycho said, "I'll tell him." He closed the door slightly because he suddenly thought the lawnmower could be heard from here.

"I didn't know he was back," the man said. "I thought he was still in America."

"He was supposed to be," Tycho said. "Okay, see you later."

"And who are you?" The man leaned forward, because Tycho had taken a step back and the door had almost swung shut.

"I'm his friend," Tycho said through the crack. "I'll pass on your message. Bye."

And click—the door closed. He leaned on the door handle and heard a soft "bye" behind the door.

H E MIGHT BE ABLE to pretend this never happened. He could fast-forward past this—as long as Oliver hadn't heard anything.

When he got back to the kitchen, he saw Oliver carrying the lawnmower into the shed. He gave him a thumbs-up and started pounding away at the ground beef again.

I T HAD BEEN A tasty meal. They were doing the dishes. Tycho had his hands in the soapy water and swirled the brush around inside the cups, over the plates, and along the insides of the pots. Oliver wandered around the kitchen, his tea towel squeezed into a glass or half-hanging over his shoulder.

Tycho knew he had to say something. Now was the time—they didn't need to look at each other, everything they said would first bounce off the kitchen tiles and the faucet, which gave the words a sense of calm and distance. Come on, tell him the trainer came by, but that you don't want this Norway Cup to . . .

"Oliver?" Tycho said.

"Yeah?"

"Um . . . Tell me about your football friends?"

"What do you want to know? They're my football buddies. It's as simple as that. When we win they're great, and when we lose I blame them."

"But isn't there anyone that you're close to? Someone you can talk to?"

"Tycho, listen. We practice and we play matches and we go to tournaments. We don't talk about life, if that's what you mean."

"Yeah, okay, but on the way to a match, don't you guys talk?"

"Sure, yeah."

"Well, what about?"

"About the game. About the competition. And"— Oliver playfully swatted at Tycho's ears with the tea towel—"about girls . . ."

"About girls?"

"Of course! About the girls in the village. What they look like . . ."

Tycho pulled his hands out of the dishwater and looked up at Oliver. The brush was dripping. "And you . . . go along with that?"

A grin spread across Oliver's face. "Maybe I'm not as loud as the others, but I do join in, yeah. I'm not going to tell them: hey, guys, can we change the subject, because I'm a soper."

Oliver had never used that word with him before, but Tycho immediately understood what it meant. It rang out across the kitchen like a gunshot, jarring and dangerous. Tycho stopped in his tracks—but then Oliver laughed, slung the tea towel around Tycho's neck, and said, "I'll never tell them that, because I'm *not* a soper. I'm with you, and you happen to be a guy. That's all."

The tea towel was moving down now, past Tycho's shoulders, past his chest. Oliver leaned over Tycho's shoulder from behind so he could still hold on to the end. At the same time, he slid his right hand past Tycho's hips, over his butt, and reached down between his legs. He grabbed the bottom end of the tea towel and pulled. The towel rubbed against Tycho's crotch. He closed his legs, trapping Oliver's hand, which started twisting and wriggling, so that Tycho almost fell over and Oliver had to catch him.

"Stop, stop!" Oliver said. "I give up!"

They both laughed. Tycho scooped up some foam, held it over Oliver's head, and said, "Enough! Promise me we'll go into town tomorrow!"

Immediately Oliver stiffened, causing Tycho to stiffen too. He lowered his foamy hand and got up, as if the referee had called a foul. Oliver got up too and straightened his T-shirt. He looked for the loop on the tea towel. When he'd finally found it, it took him a few seconds to hang it back on the hook by the sink and turn around.

"I don't think that's a good idea."

What? Tycho thought. What? Suddenly he could feel himself getting angry. No no no, he thought, if I get mad it'll all fall apart, you can't be mad at the person you're in love with. And yet he was. What did Oliver mean, not such a good idea?

"I mean—all the guys from the team are home. They're leaving for Oslo tomorrow, for the Norway Cup. What do you think is going to happen if they see me? They'll ask why I'm here. And if I'm coming."

All sorts of thoughts got tangled up in Tycho's head. So they were staying home out of self-protection!

Oliver didn't want to go to Oslo! Was that true? If it was, wasn't it better if he kept quiet about the coach's visit? Or should he tell him after all? Then why had Oliver already been to the store three times? Wouldn't it have been better for him to stay at home?

"Oliver, you know . . . this afternoon—"

Oliver interrupted him. "And what do you think will happen if they see me with you?"

Again Tycho was thrown for a loop. Again something flared up inside him. He took a breath and said, a little too loudly: "There's nothing wrong with that. Just a friend, right?"

Oliver was quiet for a moment. He walked off, out of the kitchen. But halfway he turned back and said, "Well . . . yeah . . ." He walked on, but then he turned around again. "Maybe it's me. Suddenly everything is different. It's all happening at once."

Tycho walked over to Oliver and grabbed him by the shoulders, pulling them toward him, but Oliver immediately put up his fists and boxed Tycho's arms away.

It didn't hurt, but Tycho felt his mind reeling. He searched for a way to look back, travel back in time, see what had happened. Where did it go wrong? Who was to blame? But now Oliver came toward him again. He grabbed Tycho's face, ran his fingers down his temples—down his cheeks, his lips, on which he planted a soft kiss, and then another. Finally he let go and said, "I know a movie we can watch," and before Tycho had fully recovered, they were on the sofa, the first notes of the score coming through the speakers.

"Another River Phoenix movie," Oliver said. "But a funny one this time. A comedy."

"Oh," Tycho said. "Yeah." He shook his head.

"You know what it's called?"

"No."

"*I Love You to Death.*"

THEY WATCHED FOR A minute. And another. But when the first joke came along, Tycho couldn't stand it anymore. He grabbed the remote, hit the pause button, and said, "No! We're going for a walk!"

Oliver didn't say anything. He pressed play again. Tycho leapt up, went over to the TV, and turned it off. "Come on! There's nothing wrong with you and there's nothing wrong with me. We're just friends. Can't you tell them that?"

Now Oliver jumped up too. He threw the remote onto the carpet. The cover came flying off—two batteries rolled away. The air was trembling, but Tycho thought: Don't be afraid now. Stay calm. He looked at Oliver.

Oliver looked back, his mouth taut and his eyes narrow. "No," he said.

He pushed past Tycho and headed off to his room.

Tycho followed after him. "No?" he said. "What do you mean, no?"

Oliver stopped. "We're not! 'Just friends' is exactly what we're not!" He sat down on the bed and started putting on his shoes.

"So?" Tycho said. "So what?"

But Oliver had already gotten up again and elbowed his way past Tycho, into the hallway. He walked over to the back door, crossed the yard, and went into the shed. Tycho watched him pull out his bike and throw the gate open.

GONE, TYCHO THOUGHT, HE'S gone. He ran barefoot to the front of the house, out onto the porch. Oliver was pedaling furiously down the hill. He'd almost disappeared from view. Tycho wanted to shout out, but he didn't. He ran back inside, turned the TV on, and flopped down onto the sofa. A storm was raging inside his head. He got up and gathered the parts of the remote control. He tried to put the batteries back into the case. It didn't work. He couldn't get the cover back on. He threw it back on the floor.

He went to the kitchen and searched around under the sink for something to drink. He took a swig from a bottle of wine and looked at the backyard. He would set off on foot. He had to follow Oliver. Of course. He slammed the bottle down on the counter and went to the bedroom to throw his shoes on.

H IS BAG WAS VIBRATING.
Oliver!

Tycho dug out his phone, saw that it was an unknown number, and said, "Hi!"

He heard a strange click, crackling, and then: "Tycho?"

"Mom!"

"Oh, thank goodness, honey . . ."

"Mom! What . . . how . . ."

"If only you knew . . . My God, I'm so glad—"

"I'm in Norway, Mom, you're calling Norway."

"Yes, Norway. We got your email, honey, and an email from that man, what's his name . . ."

"John."

"Yes. How are you? Are you okay? You have . . . what you wrote . . ."

It was quiet for a moment. Was she *crying*? He had to go!

"Mom! What's going on?"

"Nothing. It's nothing. You're the most precious thing I have, Tycho, you know that, don't you?"

"Mom, stop."

His father took over. "Tycho?"

"Yeah?"

"Is everything okay?"

"Yeah. Everything's great."

"You scared us, son. You barely responded to any of our messages. Just that one email . . . And you wrote that you're in love with . . . you know . . . Of course we wanted to talk to you about that, but then we read that other message, from that camp director, and all of that sounded so unlike you. So then we called that emergency number. We talked to that woman, Carol—nice lady. And now you're in Norway. How are things going over there?"

He'd already asked that. Tycho sighed.

"They're great, Dad, great."

"Good. How's your boyfriend?"

Your boyfriend!

"Oliver. Um . . . yeah, he's good too. Fine."

"Good. I'm passing you back to your mother."

"Tych, we can't talk long, because the signal keeps dropping. But we just wanted to let you know we support you. We're always behind you. It doesn't matter if you're . . ."

"Oh. Well, thanks, Mom."

"Is he a nice boy?"

"Of course."

"Are you guys on your own?"

"Yeah."

"What about his parents?"

"They're divorced. Oliver lives with his mom. But she's in Africa. On vacation."

"Oh. And when are you coming back?"

"Jeez, I don't know."

"Don't be gone too long, okay?"

"No, Mom."

"We'll have to talk more when you get home, do you understand?"

"Sure."

"Good. Oh, your father has a question. He wants to know if you have enough money."

"Yeah. Of course. In my bank account. I'm spending almost nothing here."

"Okay, good. And he wants to know if you're being careful. With sex and stuff."

"Mom, don't be stupid. Of course I am. I'll come home once you guys are back."

"Oh, great. And you're sure things are going well?"

"Yeah, everything's great."

"Well, you take care."

"Yeah, Mom, I will. Are you two having a good time?"

"Things are fine here. As usual. Now, see you soon. Bye, my sweet boy."

"Bye, Mom."

"Okay, byeee."

"Bye."

WHEN TYCHO HUNG UP, he was twice as sure that he needed to go and look for Oliver. Look for him, find him, and then everything would be okay.

Stumbling, he pulled on his shoes, flipped the key to the front door off the hook in the kitchen, and bounded down the porch steps onto the street.

A summer's evening. There was still daylight, but the dark was already rising up off the asphalt. Where would Oliver want to be found? Tycho ran through streets that he believed he remembered from a few days back. To the station. Down a shopping street. Back past the station, So far, nothing.

A new route. Through a residential neighborhood. Past a school. Nothing familiar anywhere.

After some time he glanced at his watch. How long had he been running around like this? Half an hour? Forty minutes?

He made a left turn, down a dirt road. There were fewer houses here, but then he spotted a small lit-up field at the end of the road. Of course! He couldn't believe he hadn't thought of it earlier. The football pitch! From the road he saw a brown wooden cabin. The locker rooms? The cafeteria? It was surrounded by a steel fence. Behind it, something green. Was someone there? Tycho didn't see any cars. The lights were on. The entrance gate was open. He saw a familiar bike leaning against the wall. Tycho's heart began to flutter. The door of the cabin opened. Tycho froze. An extended leg punted a ball out across the field.

Oliver.

Tycho stepped out of the shadows and wanted to say something—something important, Oliver's name —when he saw someone coming out from behind.

Someone in a tracksuit.

Someone he knew.

The trainer.

TYCHO SHRANK BACK. THE coach was dragging along a net, which he hung up on the hooks behind the nearest goalpost. Oliver helped him. They both kicked their legs to warm up their muscles. They waved their arms. They dove down to the ground and immediately pushed themselves back up again. Then the coach made a gesture. Oliver went over to the goal line and the coach started firing off shots at him. In between the thuds, Tycho heard the coach speaking softly. Maybe he was giving instructions, maybe they were compliments. But the longer they were at it, the more out of breath he and Oliver became, the harder they panted, and the quieter it got.

THE EVENING HAD TURNED grayish. Tycho stood there for a little while, invisible to the two figures in the weak glow of the streetlight. At first he just watched. Then he started thinking: Should I do something? Run out onto the pitch? Shout from the shadows that Oliver needs to come home? Softly whistle a tune? What? The Little World song? Should he go find a table in the cafeteria, wait for them to finish, and then slowly and clearly tell the coach his story?

Something was stopping him. Something got in between him and those two moving silhouettes in the distance. A red feeling. A crimson feeling that had to do with the coach's visit earlier that day. Now Oliver knew what Tycho had been keeping from him. Which meant that first of all—before anything else—Tycho would have to explain why he hadn't told him. But could it be explained? What could he say? Red shame was what he felt, throughout his body. He crept a few steps backwards and turned around. He tiptoed out through the gate and started running. He ran the whole way home.

ONCE HE GOT BACK, Tycho threw on the TV and the VHS. He didn't want to think anymore. *I Love You to Death.*

There was still wine. The movie flickered past. Tycho drank and thought: I'm the one who pushed him away. To Oslo. To that fucking Norway Cup. Right into that creep's hands.

A little later the bottle was empty. Not one drop left.

Tycho's eyes began to close. He stumbled down the hallway and fell over onto the bed. He was asleep instantly.

A NEW CHINK OF LIGHT woke him. It was dark, but the lights from the hallway cast a sharply defined disc of brightness into the room. Oliver? Tycho rubbed his eyes and looked for the green digits of the clock on the desk: 0:42. He dropped his head back onto the pillow and listened to the sounds. He heard shoes. The sucking noise of a door opening. Rummaging. Footsteps in the hallway. And suddenly, right up close, a click. More light. Oliver was shining a flashlight into his face.

"Wake up!"

"Oliver?"

Oliver leaned over and stroked Tycho's neck with a warm hand. Tycho smelled his sweat.

"Let me show you around Gjøvik."

Tycho rolled over. Holy shit, his head.

Oliver beckoned. "Come on!"

Groaning, Tycho got up. At the end of the hallway he saw the open door, the steps that led down the porch, down the little path, down the hill, into town.

A little later they were walking side by side. Tycho felt his headache slowly drifting away, almost out of reach. He saw the town at his feet. They walked and walked, not saying anything. Every now and then motion lights flashed on outside houses, or they'd hear something scampering away in the undergrowth. Here and there, what looked like a rag could be seen flapping on a clothesline in the wind. They walked and walked. Squares, gardens, silent cars, meadows, rocks.

They came to the edge of Gjøvik. Here there was no fence holding them in. There was no minimum age for being outside. No Little World. Maybe everything will be okay, Tycho thought.

They climbed up mountain paths, they held each other and wrapped their arms around each other, until they stopped somewhere, looked around, and finally sank to the ground. They sat and squinted along pointed fingers at their own backyard. Tycho gazed at it all. This was what he'd wanted. This was what days should be like. Or nights.

But words were in the way. There was something that still needed to be said.

O LIVER BEGAN.
"Sometimes you can only do one thing at a time," he said. Then he went back to looking ahead.

"What do you mean?" Tycho asked after a little while.

Oliver turned to face him. "I want to be with you," he said, "but I also want to go to Oslo."

Tycho felt something beginning to throb behind

his temples. His headache flaring up again? Shame? Suddenly he took a breath and said, "I think you should go." I have no choice, he thought, there's nothing else I can say.

Oliver was quiet.

After some time he said, "Do you really mean that?"

"Yes," Tycho said.

"But what about you?"

"I'll stay here. It's just a few days, right?"

"Three. Five, if we win." Oliver's voice sounded cautiously hopeful, almost happy.

Tycho said, "Or I'll come with you."

Immediately he saw Oliver dropping his shoulders.

"See, that's what I'm trying to say," Oliver said. "Some things just don't go together."

For a moment something flared up inside Tycho, a fire with tiny black sparks, but the headache held it at bay. He sighed. "I get it," he said. "You can't explain this to your football friends."

Oliver got up, went and stood behind him, and placed his hands on Tycho's shoulders. He bent over, kissed his ears and the top of his head, and said, "That's exactly it. You're unexplainable. Thank you."

Tycho took Oliver's hands, let him pull him up, and said, "Hey, about your coach . . ."

Oliver put three fingers on his mouth. "Don't say it," he said, "it's history. Let's go to bed."

"Okay," Tycho said.

"But quick," Oliver said. "Very quick."

A S THEY HURRIED BACK, Tycho's mind raced. Was this how things were supposed to go? Which one of them had given in? He was startled by that thought. Given in? He and Oliver—this shouldn't be a competition.

It's not supposed to be a competition, Tycho thought—but by then they were already standing next to the bed and Oliver's fingers, quick and soft and prodding, were sliding down his naked, defenseless back.

S HOULD I PACK MY Little World shirt?" Oliver asked from the bedroom.

"If you want," Tycho said. He was frying eggs. The whites were running together. Tycho noticed, pushed the yolks to the middle, and stirred them in.

He'd jolted awake at least five times that night. He'd look over to the side, blinking, see Oliver, and feel the sudden impulse to shake him. There was something he still needed to tell him—no, ask him. What exactly he wasn't sure, but his hands had already slipped out from beneath the sheets and were hovering half an inch from Oliver's shoulder. But then they sank down again and Tycho folded them back alongside his own body. The words he'd woken up with had scattered on the wind, and you couldn't ask a question when the words had all blown away.

So he sank back against the pillow and just looked at Oliver sleeping. He thought: So beautiful. And then: He'll be gone tomorrow. And finally he pictured himself, how he'd lie here, all alone, in a dark room where he wouldn't be able to conjure up anything familiar.

"No," Tycho said, and he looked out the window, at the sun. When it first appeared early that morning, finally, after all that worrying, he suddenly knew he had to decide something. That he shouldn't just lie there and wait for things to happen. That he needed to take action. After that, he'd dropped his self-pitying thoughts.

He'd gotten up and pulled the schedule for the Norway Cup out of Oliver's coat pocket. He'd copied what he wanted to know onto a piece of paper and then crept back to bed.

"Do you know where my shoes are?"

T HE KETTLE WAS WHISTLING. Tycho threw a tea bag into the pot, poured water over it, and waited. Then he tugged at the string, lowered it, repeated that a few times, and filled two cups halfway. He grabbed the milk from the fridge and watched with satisfaction as the creamy white mixed with the reddish brown of the tea.

Oliver sat down at the table. "Are you sure you're letting me go?"

"Yes," Tycho said. "Here, have some tea."

"Thanks. And I don't need to worry about you?"

"No," Tycho said.

"I'll call you every day. Whenever I can."

"Mmh."

"Will you keep your phone on?"

"Okay."

"In case of emergency."

"Mmh."

"Cause you can't call me when I'm with the guys."

"Hm."

"You understand that, don't you?"

Tycho nodded. Just go, he thought, just you wait and see.

O LIVER'S DEPARTURE WAS HERALDED by the sound of car tires. The crunching of gravel. Honking and an engine that idled for a while. "I have to go," he said.

For a moment it seemed like he was regretting his decision. Like he was about to say: "I'm not going. Let them honk. Let them wait outside the door." He put the bag he'd already picked up back down again, turned to Tycho, and wrapped his arms around him. Tycho was startled—suddenly he felt like prying Oliver's fingers off his back and telling him, "Come on, off you go," but he resisted it and parted his lips. Oliver pulled his mouth toward his, kissing Tycho as if he was trying to suck out a fire from somewhere inside him.

Then he let go and said, "Hey, thank you," picked up his stuff, headed for the door, and turned around one more time. "Okay, I'm going," he said again.

Tycho raised his hand.

He thought: So am I.

WHEN THE DOOR HAD closed and he'd heard the car drive away, he went into the living room, pulled out the piece of paper with the match schedule copied on it, sat down, and started planning. In the past, all sorts of events had beckoned him and he'd just followed along, nodding meekly, but now that time was over. Now he had to be the one to decide on the course of things. How? He wasn't quite sure. But he knew one thing. He wanted to see Oliver again, before the day was over. In Oslo.

THE HOURS BEFORE IT was time to leave were light and exciting. He shopped for food. He withdrew cash. He strolled through the town one more time. He took Oliver's bike out, because he had so much energy he felt like riding up steep hills. When he got back home he jumped in the shower. With the water blasting his back he felt strong and fit, despite having barely slept, despite all the exertion.

It was almost time to head for the station. He put a few last things away. He picked up the outdoor furniture and carried it back into the shed. Tycho saw how everything was in its right place—the lawnmower and the snow shovel and the rake and the bicycles, all neatly lined up. For a moment he thought: Why do I have to go shaking everything up if Oliver likes order?

Ten more minutes. He did a final walk-through of the house. Everything was ready. He was all packed. One last quick look in the hallway. Oliver's desk. The shower.

Suddenly he was outside Stina's room. He opened the door. A bed with a red quilt. Two lamps. Books. A wardrobe. A poster of a summer dance in a country village: farm girls twirling in men's arms. The room smelled of vanilla. There was a ripped pair of pantyhose underneath the vanity. On the bedside table there was a picture of Oliver. It must have been taken recently: Oliver in a rowboat, without a shirt on. The sun was shining. He was holding a fishing rod and grinning with white teeth. Tycho picked up the frame. For a moment he thought: Everything is long over. Oliver has already left, his father is somewhere up north,

Stina is on a different continent, and I'm here, in a house that isn't mine. For all of us, Oliver is just a picture.

But then he thought: Oh, stop whining and get going.

THROUGH THE TOURIST INFORMATION office at the station he'd managed to book a room in a youth hostel. He'd dropped off his suitcase there and studied a map of Oslo. They'd given him directions and now he was standing in a tram on his way to the Ekebergsletta field. The first matches were already under way. He was surrounded by football teams. Girls, boys, all wearing the same tracksuits. On the back, below the club name, they said, NORGE, DAN-MARK, SCOTLAND, or SUISSE. Tycho held on to a pole and smiled. Like the stainless steel beneath his fingers—that's how strong he wanted his conviction to be. His belief that he was doing the right thing.

ALL OVER THE SITE, clumps of football players were following along behind their trainers. There were chants, flags waving in the air, and upbeat music on top of all the other noise. Tycho went to the information booth and asked where the Gjøvik team was playing. Pitch 17. He followed the signs and saw a crowd gathered around the pitch. He came closer and peered over someone's shoulder, searching for the goalies.

There! Over there on the left was Oliver, his strong legs in shiny black pants. His jersey was purple. The gloves he was wearing made his fingers look even longer. Tycho shivered.

He walked down the side of the pitch to the goal. Oliver hadn't noticed him yet, but then how could he? There were people in the way, pressed up behind the perimeter rope. Tycho elbowed his way to the front, until he was almost standing behind Oliver. That slender back. On his jersey, in sky blue, was the number 1.

Suddenly there was a roar. A group of forwards were charging toward the goal like a combine harvester. Three, four people, the ball flying along at their feet. Failed tackles, one after the other, defenders crashing onto the grass to left and right. Oliver made himself wide. He raised his arms to block the shot that was coming his way, to intimidate his opponents, to say: Look, I'm standing here and I've got quick reflexes. But it was too late. He thrust out his left leg, but the ball slammed into the netting, into a corner that was just out of reach. People cheered, people sighed: "Aahh . . ."

Oliver got up and threw a clod of dirt. He walked back into the goal, bent over to grab the ball, straightened up again—and looked straight into Tycho's eyes.

Tycho flinched. Oliver flinched too. For a moment his movements slowed down, but then he regained his composure. He gave a curt nod, turned around, and with a sharp kick sent the ball flying back to the center circle.

N OT LONG AFTER, THE game ended. Gjøvik won, despite the goal they'd conceded. Tycho saw Oliver being mobbed by his defenders. He shook the referee's hand and gave the captain of the losing team a pat on the shoulder. Tycho walked along the sideline, until somewhere halfway down the pitch he got close to Oliver. He tried to think of something to say, something quick, something that summarized the whole speech he had prepared in just one word, but Oliver beat him to it. He darted a quick look at Tycho and said: "The stage." Then he shook a few of the other players' hands and walked away. Tycho saw them all leave the pitch, flowing together into one warm rivulet of sweat.

The stage?

T HE STAGE WAS SOMEWHERE on the edge of the site. This was where the opening ceremony of the tournament had taken place and where the closing ceremony would be held in a few days' time. A thicket of tall green bushes surrounded an outdoor stage with a tarp roof, and the bleachers were concealed behind more greenery. The perfect place to meet. The football hubbub could be heard from all directions, but the stage was deserted. Tycho sat down cross-legged on the wooden boards and waited. He told himself it was all going according to plan. First he had to be in Oslo. Then it needed to get too late for him to go back to Gjøvik. He had to show Oliver that he didn't want to spend a day in this country without him. He wondered when Oliver was going to turn up.

After fifteen minutes he had to get up because his feet were getting numb. He walked around the podium, looked out onto the practice pitches from the entrance to the site, and then decided to sit back down again.

It took a long time. Tycho grew angry at himself because he'd started craving a Coke. That wasn't what he'd come here for. He was here for bluegrass love. He whispered it softly to himself: bluegrass love. Suddenly he felt his heart pounding, knocking all the things he wanted to say to Oliver sideways.

Somewhere in the distance, a shrill whistle signaled a foul.

F INALLY, FINALLY, OLIVER, HAIR wet from the shower, his arms swinging slightly, emerged from between the bleachers and headed straight toward

Tycho. He was wearing a tracksuit. His shoes tapped against the path. The steps led him up to the podium: one, two, three. For half a second he blocked Tycho's sun, then he turned around and sat down. Now all the light fell onto and around the two of them.

They looked at each other.

Oliver looked away. Then Tycho did too.

They took a breath, started talking at the same time, and then fell silent again.

"You go first," Oliver said.

"No. You," said Tycho.

They both laughed, cautiously.

"Okay," Oliver said. He stared at the ground. "Are you here because of me?"

"Yeah, of course."

"Are you staying over?"

"I've got a hotel."

Tycho gave him a sidelong glance. Oliver was gently shaking his head. Off in the distance, people were singing a football song.

"When did you come up with this idea?"

"Last night. I couldn't sleep."

"Why didn't you say anything?"

"You would have stopped me."

"I wouldn't have left."

"Why?"

"If I'd thought you wanted me to stay."

"But didn't you want to go?"

"I don't know. You're confusing me."

"Really?"

"You keep confusing me."

AFTER SOME TIME TYCHO asked, "So now what?"

"I don't know. I have to get back. We're going out to dinner with the team."

"And then what?"

"We don't have anything planned after that. They may be going out."

"I'm in the youth hostel. Room 212."

"Maybe I'll come and see you later."

"Should I come to dinner?"

"No! It's bad enough the coach saw you just now!"

Oliver got up. Tycho looked up at him. Oliver stood in front of him like a statue, black, with the sun like a wreath around his head. A group of girls were approaching. They walked over to one of the bleachers.

"So are you coming tonight?" Tycho asked.

"Yeah," Oliver said, "maybe. If I can get away. I have to get back now."

Tycho got up too and held out his hand. As if there was an agreement that had to be sealed. He didn't dare ask for a kiss.

Oliver briefly stroked his fingertips and walked away.

SOMEWHERE HALFWAY DOWN KARL Johans gate, the main street that runs through the center of Oslo, Tycho was sitting on the grass, his fingers splayed on the ground behind him, his legs sticking out in front. Cars were driving by, and trams, but Tycho was watching someone who'd climbed onto a plinth and then stopped moving. Whenever a bystander dropped coins into the box at his feet, the man, who was spray-painted gold, would hinge forward from the hips and tip his golden hat by way of thanks. In between the man's bows, Tycho tried to figure out what he was going to say that evening. He didn't want to be unhappy about how things had gone at the tournament. He had revealed his presence. He'd talked to Oliver, and Oliver had talked to him, and now he was confused.

That's good, Tycho thought, that's good. That's how it begins. And then . . .

Yes, and then what?

His arms had started tingling—he'd been leaning back for too long. He got up and watched a little girl pretend to throw money into the golden man's cashbox. The man wasn't fooled. He didn't bow for air.

TWO, THREE MORE HOURS. Tycho walked down Karl Johans gate. At a newsstand he saw Dutch newspapers. He considered buying one, but didn't. Holland was much too far away. Somewhere in a back street near the port he looked in the window of a tattoo shop. Maybe he should mark the moment. Have some symbol inked in. Something that would stay forever.

He walked on. A little further along he went into a shabby music store and started rifling through a rack of CDs. After a while he noticed the *tick-tick-tick* of the CD cases hitting each other, like seconds flying by, like he was counting back in time, and a moment later he suddenly decided there was something he wanted to find—and had before that night. When the first rack had turned up nothing, he moved on to a second and a third. It wasn't until the last one that he found what he was looking for: a CD of bluegrass music. The soundtrack to being in love.

He asked if he could listen to it, and he knew immediately that everything was right: the sparks came flying out of the headphones. He started getting hot. That evening in the barbecue joint came rushing back into his ears, and as the rhythm reached fever pitch, so did his expectations: when he heard this, Oliver would . . .

Oliver would . . .

He would . . .

He glanced up at the clock that hung in the store.

Shit!

He had to grab some dinner!

And get back to his room!

T HE NORWAY CUP WAS everywhere. Tycho was sitting downstairs, in the lounge, and every-where he looked he saw letters on tracksuits. Even the men and women he thought were random tourists at first were carrying bags with little plastic football trophies on the zippers. The TV overhead was show-ing the opening ceremony: boys and girls, hand in hand. Heads held high and someone giving a speech in front of a flag. Little World, Tycho thought, and checked his phone for the twelfth time.

They must have had dinner by now. Oliver might be here any minute now.

He chewed off a piece of his fingernail. His hands smelled of hotel soap. After wolfing down half a pizza in the restaurant on the corner, he'd run back up to his room, taking the stairs two at a time.

He'd sat down, ready, waiting. On the bed at first, then on a chair by the window. Then back on the bed.

It was taking longer than he'd expected and Oliver still hadn't turned up, so he looked for a way to pass the time. He studied the CD booklet: lyrics about love.

He put the CD back on the table and returned to the window.

After another half hour, he went to the communal bathroom, which was in the hallway. He left a note on the door to his room: *Be right back. In the shower.* He hoped that Oliver would walk in as he was stretching out his arms to let the water wash over his entire body. That Oliver would look at him, just like he'd looked at Oliver, in America, when everything had begun in that unexpected slant of light and water. He wrapped his phone in his towel—it had to be close by, but it couldn't get wet. He took his clothes off. His skin started tingling. He even left the door slightly ajar so Oliver would be able to get a first glimpse through the crack.

OLIVER HADN'T COME. THEY must be getting a late dinner—he was probably just a little delayed. Tycho got dressed, splashed a little extra aftershave on, and then went to sit on the bed again. But soon he'd run back downstairs—what if Oliver had forgotten his room number?

TIME IS TOUGH WHEN you need to get through it somehow. Tycho was just sitting there, downstairs in the lounge, where everyone had already come and gone at least three times. Everything was moving, but at the same time everything was standing still. And because nothing seemed to be happening, his mind couldn't help but return to the events of the past few weeks. His eyes were looking for Oliver's form, but his thoughts were back at Amsterdam airport, and in Knoxville, in their supply closet, on the track, on the hill in Norway, on the train, and here.

It was as if he was being taken by the hand to see it all happening again. But this time he could also see he still hadn't done enough. That he'd just been trailing along after everything. That he'd been running himself silly, like a stupid fullback.

WHEN HE REALIZED THAT, he got up. He walked outside and pulled out his phone. Shaking with determination, he looked for Oliver's name in his contacts. Hit the call button. Heard the ringing, three, four times. Then: laughter and loud voices and a shouted "Hello?"

"Hi," Tycho said, "it's me."

"What? I can't—"

"You have to come here."

"I can't hear you. What?"

"Can you still come by tonight?"

There was singing in the background, loud and off-key. Someone shouted something.

"Be quiet a sec! What? Tonight?"

"Dammit, Oliver, you said you'd stop by."

"Yeah, I can't talk right now."

"Well, when *can* you talk?"

"I'll call you later."

"Dammit, Oliver."

"What?"

Tycho hung up.

TYCHO STOOD IN THE middle of the room, his hands squeezed into dumbbells. He'd shoved the door open and let it slam shut behind him. His heart was pounding. So this is it, he thought. He's gone. It was finished—he was gone. He went over to the sink and threw his toothbrush, toothpaste, and the bar of soap into his toiletry bag. He zipped it shut and hurled it into his open suitcase. Then he looked around, but all of the objects in the room seemed too calm and unassuming to be mad at. Until his eyes fell on the CD. In one furious motion he grabbed the case off the table, broke it open, kicked at the disc as it fell to the floor, and twisted the plastic with both hands. It snapped in two with a loud crack.

Broken, Tycho thought, and he fell back onto the bed. Gone. Broken. He was panting, his arms lying limp at his sides. The shards slipped from his fingers and dropped to the floor. He hugged his knees and curled into a ball.

He stared at the CD booklet lying on the table. The sight of it almost made him cry—it looked so alone.

A FTER A WHILE HIS eyes closed. He was jerked awake by one last thought. What if Oliver really didn't have a choice? What if he had a reason for not showing up? But then he sank back into the covers and fell asleep.

T HE SMELL OF ALCOHOL mixed with the darkness. Tycho dreamt that he was riding in a carriage. It was hot and a little uncomfortable, because his foot seemed to be trapped. And then there was that smell.

But the carriage came to a halt. Suddenly he was lying somewhere and it was dark all around him. His eyes pricked open a little wider and he saw Oliver's silhouette, sitting on the bed beside him.

Tycho jolted awake and sat up. His foot came free.

There was Oliver. His head was bowed, his tracksuit jacket hung from his shoulders. He didn't even look over when he started talking.

"The door was open," he said.

"Oh," Tycho said.

"It's late," Oliver said, "and I have practice again at ten tomorrow morning. This is my world, Tycho.

You're far away from home. No one's got their eye on you."

Tycho pulled up his knees and was about to say something, but suddenly Oliver leaned in toward him and said "Sorry" in a strange voice, "Tycho, sorry," and moved his mouth to Tycho's lips.

Tycho let it wash over him. The taste of beer in his mouth and the safe loop of Oliver's arms around him made him forget what he'd been about to say. Oliver sat up, rose to his feet, kicked off his shoes, and took off his jacket and pants and T-shirt, his arms flailing.

He jumped back onto the bed, unbuttoned Tycho's shirt, and helped him out of the rest of his clothes.

I T WAS MORNING AND Tycho opened his eyes. No one next to him. No clothes on the floor. His own pants and socks slung over the back of the chair in a way he recognized—but not as his own. He sat up and looked. It didn't even look that different, and yet it felt unmistakably altered, tinged with a good kind of dirty. Oliver had been here. And as he thought that, he felt it in his own body, his skin, his mouth, and his lips. See? he thought. See? He *had* shown up.

He threw the sheet off his legs and got up. Lying on the table was the CD case, the shards picked up and pieced back together.

When he saw that, Tycho quickly pulled on his clothes and hurried out the door.

WITH HIS TRAM PASS still in his hand, he ran out onto the practice ground. A game was already under way. Boys in yellow vests playing against boys without yellow vests. Tycho counted. Seven against seven, on half a pitch, with both sides shooting at the same goal. The coach was gesturing from the sideline. Oliver was in goal. He dipped in and out of the game and was even able to give Tycho a quick sidelong greeting. Some of the boys shot a quick look his way.

The morning sun was already blazing. Tycho took off his jacket, spread it on the ground, and sat down. He inhaled, breathing in the smell of grass and morning air. This is going to be a good day, he thought. Today it will all work out. Suddenly one guy made a great pass. One of his teammates got on the end of it and pressed forward, but Oliver made a dive and deflected the shot. The defenders gave Oliver a quick hug. Hey, Tycho thought, hey. Well, all right then. Just for a moment. He smiled cheerfully at the pitch.

Soon after, the game glitched and ground to a halt. From all over the field the boys jogged in and converged on one point. Someone was lying in the penalty area. Tycho hadn't been paying attention. Who was it? Not

Oliver—he was crouching by the person's side. The coach gingerly turned one of the boy's feet from side to side. Then he looked up and called something out to Oliver. Oliver hung his head. A few of the other guys looked away, into the distance. The coach got up and addressed his team. Oliver helped the injured player off the pitch. He slung the guy's arm around his own shoulder and together they stumbled over to the first-aid station. The coach glanced around. He picked a yellow vest up off the ground and walked off with it. He came back soon afterwards, the vest still in his hand. The players were standing around waiting. One guy was resting his foot on the ball.

Suddenly the coach was jogging across the field to Tycho. He came up to him and said, "Hello again. We need a substitute for a minute."

Tycho hurriedly got up. "But I'm not a football player."

"That's okay, it's just a practice game. Just go to the back and try to stop anything that comes your way. Show us what you've got. Come on. Hurry up." The coach handed him the yellow vest, and before Tycho knew what was happening, he'd taken it and pulled it over his shoulders. He ran after the coach onto the pitch. A few of the guys nodded and Tycho looked around for his position. The coach himself went and stood in goal. Oliver wasn't back yet.

THE PITCH WAS AN expanse of empty space. Tycho walked and walked. He chased down every ball. Before long, he was sweating in his vest, but it didn't bother him. He felt free—a breeze was blowing around him, and it seemed like he could run a whole week's stiffness from being cooped up indoors out of his body in one go. Every now and then someone would yell something at him, something he didn't understand, and he'd say "yes!", nod, and run twice as fast.

Oliver had come back from the first-aid station. Tycho was busy marking an attacker and saw Oliver looking at him, then over at the trainer, who sauntered across to the sideline nodding, and then back at him. Tycho felt that look propelling him forward. It was as if new blood was rushing through his body, pure energy that made him run, turn, duck, until the coach came up to him and gestured for him to slow down. "Okay," Tycho panted, "okay."

But he couldn't. Here he was, among Oliver's friends, at Oliver's tournament, one world united with the other, all was well and no one batted an eyelid at his presence. A ball appeared at his feet, and suddenly he saw a gap. Tycho ran at it and the ball stayed glued to his feet. He closed in on the goal and took a shot. He was shooting at Oliver, who was so startled, he'd been way too late getting back in goal, and now made a last-ditch attempt at a save by diving backwards. But he could see the ball escaping, the ball Tycho had shot, rolling into the goal.

T YCHO JUMPED INTO THE air and cheered. The guys around him started laughing, because the rule was that the ball had to go back to the center line before anyone could score. But Tycho wasn't paying them any attention. Oliver was still lying on the ground and Tycho ran over to him, sliding along the grass next to him on his front like he'd seen on television. He wanted to throw his arms around Oliver to celebrate this triumph, to celebrate that everything was glorious now, anything was possible now—but then a sharp whistle rang out across the pitch.

Tycho looked up and so did Oliver. He'd half-gotten up and turned away from Tycho. It was as if they'd been frozen, put on pause. Who had whistled and why?

It was the coach, who was gesturing wildly.

"Kjelsberg! Over here! And bring your partner."

Tycho pushed himself up on his elbows and scrambled to his feet. Oliver got up too. The rest of the field was quiet. All of Oliver's fellow players seemed too surprised to move. The ball was lying abandoned in the goal. The coach started walking, and Oliver and Tycho followed him.

"I need to have a word with you," the coach barked

at Tycho, when they stopped a little further on. "Over there!" He gestured toward a wooden shed that was serving as a dugout. "One moment."

He indicated with an abrupt jerk of his hand that Oliver had to come along first. As they walked off, Tycho saw the arm that the coach put around Oliver's shoulders. And beneath it, Oliver's body, letting itself be ushered along.

HOW LONG DID HE stand there? Why did he keep standing there? The wind picked up. His sweat dried. Maybe he'd gone too far. But Oliver? Oliver?

OLIVER APPEARED AROUND THE corner of the wooden shed. His head hanging way too low, his black hair hanging too loose, he came toward Tycho. "Are you coming?"

"What did he say to you? Oliver, what did he say? We can still leave, Oliver, you and me. Just get out of here!"

But they were already in front of the dugout.

The coach was sitting on the bench and motioned for them to sit down too.

I UNDERSTAND EVERYTHING," HE SAID. "And there's no problem whatsoever. You and Oliver, that's not a problem. But I've known Oliver since he was ten years old. And I know his mother. And I know what he wants. For a moment, I thought he'd given it all up because he went to America, but just this week he's convinced me that the opposite is true. He wants to be discovered. And he can be. At this tournament. There are scouts here, they'll be watching him. It's not too late, but it will be if he keeps getting distracted. By you, Tie-ko. By his personal life. Which shouldn't be a problem, of course, don't get me wrong. And there isn't a problem. But sports and being gay—"

Suddenly Tycho was shouting over the coach's words. He jumped up and yelled: "Then why don't you shut up? Just shut up, man!" He ran out of the dugout and bolted off.

Several strides away, the other boys were waiting. They were sitting on the field, crouching or standing with their hands on their hips. Tycho slowed down. With a furious motion he tried to yank the yellow vest over his head, but he couldn't get it off.

He was about to walk on, but then he heard his name.

"Tycho!"

He turned around. His boyfriend was standing in front of the dugout.

Oliver put a hand up to shield his eyes from the sun and looked.

Tycho looked back.

Oliver tucked his black hair behind his ears.

Tycho lowered his shoulders.

Oliver was still looking.

Tycho was still looking back.

B UT JUST AS TYCHO was about to walk back over to Oliver and say something—something that would undo everything after all, something that would erase all the chaotic events of the previous fifteen minutes and replace them with one simple, glowing conclusion—right at that moment the coach came and stood next to Oliver and put a hand on his forearm.

S LOW-MO REPLAY
Tycho Zeling starts to move. The edge of his T-shirt flaps in the wind, his hair is sticking up wildly, his arms and legs are chopping through the air and his feet are pounding the grass. He sprints ahead—even in slow motion, he's fast—straight at the two people in front of him. Now the guys behind him start moving too, more slowly, but all at the same time. Someone is limping up to them from the left with a bandaged foot—by chance? Yes, by chance. But Tycho Zeling bends forward at the waist—how much time has passed? Two seconds, maybe three—and Tycho Zeling

slams his head into someone's stomach. Maybe the man in the tracksuit was the intended victim, but due to an odd shift in position—we can't see right now whose, Tycho Zeling's or his goalkeeper boyfriend's—the angry head ends up cannoning into Oliver Kjelsberg's stomach instead. In any case, both boys tumble onto the ground and roll over several times. The others gather around them and watch.

I T WAS AS IF Tycho was trying to beat something into him. The courage of his convictions. As if his fingers were trying to claw a verdict into Oliver's back. As if his muscles wanted to press it into Oliver's body: We have to be together! We have to disappear into each other! The two of us should be one champion's body, goddammit! Around them Tycho heard shouting, shouting he didn't understand, but amid all that noise Oliver got closer and closer and Tycho felt that he had the strength to make him understand everything. As long as Oliver didn't back down. As long as he kept fighting too. They rolled around and around and around—now Tycho was the one on top, now it was Oliver, now Tycho again.

U NTIL SUDDENLY OLIVER WENT limp. Until Tycho looked up at Oliver's face and saw that he'd given up. Tycho had won. Tycho had lost. It was all over now. There was nothing more he could do. Oliver had given up. Oliver was gone.

Tycho's knees pressed into the grass—he was still straddling Oliver's felled body. Their lower bodies were touching and Tycho's hands were pinning back Oliver's wrists. Oliver had a halo of matted black hair.

Tycho looked and Oliver looked. And there was nothing. Nothing left in their gaze.

UNTIL TYCHO LEANED IN after all. A new impulse rose up from somewhere inside him. For a moment it looked like he was going to lie on top of Oliver, but he didn't. Instead he puckered his lips and gave him a kiss. His lips touched against Oliver's.

And Oliver lay there, frozen in shock.

OLIVER WAS STUNNED. AN ugly scratch passed over his face, like when a child scores out a ruined drawing.

For a moment Tycho was happy. Now he'd really won.

But then the shock caught up with him.

It had grown quiet around them. Everyone was holding their breath. Oliver's eyes seemed several shades whiter. His pupils wcre narrower than ever.

S UDDENLY TYCHO PANICKED. HE felt his face growing hot and he could only think of one way out. One move that would wipe away Oliver's shame and his own betrayal, but at the same time, would mark the end of the promise this day had held, the hope he'd felt when he left Gjøvik, the goal he'd set himself.

H E LEANED IN CLOSE and whispered, "Spit." When Oliver didn't seem to understand what he meant, Tycho let go of his wrists and said, "Spit in my face. Now. Hard. Then they'll think what you want them to think."

O LIVER GOT UP ON one elbow, looked at Tycho as if begging for forgiveness, and before abruptly breaking free and walking off, he rounded his mouth into a circle, gathered the spit that was laced with the fire of their three weeks together, puckered his lips like Tycho had done, and spat straight ahead.

IT HURT LIKE HELL. But then it was supposed to. Tycho snuck a glance past his upper arm at the mirror. Swollen red edges.

He'd managed to find the tattoo shop again. The owner was in and had mumbled for him to sit down.

The machine was humming. Tiny needles pricked ink into his skin. Slowly the drawing appeared, blood oozing from the lines. The tattoo artist snorted. He'd shown him other designs, much bigger, much more interesting, but Tycho wanted this one.

The tattoo artist grabbed a cotton ball and rubbed his arm. He was about to bandage the tattoo, but hesitated and asked, "No name?" Tycho thought for a moment, but then he shook his head and said, "No, no name."

HOW STRANGE THAT THE trams were still running. That tourists were sitting outside restaurants ordering slices of pizza. That the pigeons were still as brazen as ever. That everything still kept going, even though Tycho had stopped the turning of the days.

He had no other choice. He had no choice but to

book a return flight. He'd gone from the football ground back to the hotel. On the way there his mind was blank. He'd touched his lips. And when he got off the tram, the summer breeze had brushed his cheek, and he'd thought: Spit dries. Ink doesn't.

During the night, again and again he saw Oliver's face—all twisted up, helpless. He was convinced he'd destroyed everything. That he should never have been running around in Oliver's world in the first place. The big world, the little world. If your life was the sum total of all your decisions, then how was it possible that when you had to make the biggest decision of all, you felt like you didn't know what you were doing? That when it really came down to it, you were sure you didn't *have* a choice—and then just watched yourself doing the wrong thing.

H E'D SKIPPED BREAKFAST. HE wouldn't be able to keep anything down. He walked around town and spotted the golden man, who was still standing on his plinth. He didn't understand how anyone was capable of that. How you could just do nothing when everyone else was doing all sorts of things. How you could stand still when everything around you was moving somewhere. How, when someone tried to make contact by tossing a coin your way, you could just give them the same spiel every time, bowing politely—no, disdainfully, as if you were only coming closer so they could really see the way you looked down on the world from up there. Tycho wasn't like that. He hadn't kept his distance. He'd gotten carried away by everything that happened to him in the little world, in the big world. He was no hunter. He was no golden man. But then what was he?

Just keep walking, he thought, don't stand still now.

HE FELT HIS UPPER arm. This will stay, he thought. This is permanent now. This ink isn't going anywhere. This would remind him of these days.

He wouldn't be seeing Oliver again.

BUT WHEN HE ARRIVED back at the hotel to get his things, the receptionist said someone had asked for him. A boy his age. He'd been calling all afternoon.

When Tycho got upstairs the first thing he did was check his phone. Which was off. Dead battery. He plugged in his charger and could hardly wait for the screen to light up. Seven missed calls. All from Oliver.

As he was clicking them away to see if there were messages too, Oliver called again.

Tycho answered, shaking.

"Hello?"

"Tycho, can I still see you?"

Tycho was unable to speak. He opened his mouth, but couldn't remember how it worked—talking.

With a jolt, the air came hurtling back into his lungs. "Tonight?" he asked, his voice hoarse. "Tonight at the station. Before I head out to the airport?"

H E BOUGHT A DUTCH newspaper and sat down on a bench in the concourse. He stretched out his legs, then tucked them back underneath him.

The paper said that Ajax had sold their goalie.

T HERE ARE FISH THAT fire jets of water at the insects they're preying on. That's pretty much the way that Tycho was looking around the station right now. As if his eyes could fire tractor beams that could grab hold of Oliver. Oliver Kjelsberg. The boy he knew and didn't know at all. Suddenly a panicked thought flashed through his head: What if I've already forgotten what he looks like?

But suddenly he looked up, and froze. There he was. More familiar than he'd been at the airport and that time in the shower, more familiar than the day before, lying underneath him, battle-spent. His tracksuit in the crowd. The familiar gesture of him tucking his hair behind his ears as he stood there scanning the heads. Looking for him. Tycho felt a pang, and not just in his upper arm—a desperate sense of wanting everything to keep going, or start over if need be, like on a roller coaster that you've spent ages waiting in line for.

I can pull up my hood and hide, Tycho thought. I can fly away. I can stay another six days. Get up. Sit down. Attack. Defend.

He raised his hand.

Hey," Tycho said, once Oliver was in front of him.

"Hey," Oliver said, and sat down next to him.

Everything that had happened hung in the air between them. A curtain of complications. A wall of fog that they suddenly found they could talk through.

Tycho began. "Ajax is looking for a goalie."

"Hmm. I played badly."

"Did you lose?"

"No, we did win. We're in the finals."

"Did you see any scouts?"

"No, no interest, the coach says."

Another pang. "Let's not talk about the coach."

"Yeah, okay."

"What should we talk about?"

"Dunno."

"Did the guys say anything?"

"They're avoiding me."

"Oh. I'm sorry."

"That's the least of my worries."

Tycho hesitated, but he knew he had to ask. "Are you mad? I totally messed everything up."

"You? No, no, no, *I'm* the one who . . . are you still mad?"

"Me? At you?"

Oliver didn't answer. They each stood in silence. Tycho looked around awkwardly. So many people. Oliver looked too. He nodded toward the platforms off to the side. "When do you have to go?"

"In a minute."

AND SUDDENLY TYCHO THOUGHT: Maybe it's the golden man who moves. Everyone else goes with the flow, because it's easy to just keep chugging along. Trailing along after something, letting things run their course, that's easy. But standing still, ultimately that's a decision too. A silent movement— against time.

He turned to Oliver. "It doesn't end here. I don't want to forget you."

Oliver turned red—something Tycho hadn't seen before.

"Look," Tycho said. He scrunched up the sleeve of his T-shirt and pulled off the bandage.

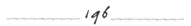

Oliver looked. He leaned in. With soft fingers, with the wind in his fingers, he traced the bloody lines.

"An airplane," he whispered, "an airplane with a banner."

He crinkled his eyes. A broad grin lit up his entire face. And then he said, with a new, unfamiliar quiver in his voice: "Of course it doesn't end here. Where did you get that tattoo? I want the address."

AUTHOR'S NOTE

When I wrote *The Days of Bluegrass Love,* I was in a constant fever. It was one of my first books and I didn't really know what I was doing. Tycho and Oliver had appeared inside me—they were calling the shots. I followed them with my pen, so fast I felt like I was burning up. It was 1998. Up until that point I'd only published a handful of children's books, most of them poetry. But I found myself yearning for a book that gave a visceral, first-person account of a love sparking between two boys. Until that point, the queer books I'd read—if I could even find any—had mostly been tragic: death and heartbreak were never far away. Now I wanted to write the kind of book I wished had been around fifteen years earlier, a book like a warm glow, a book in which many shots get fired, though they never hit love itself. The romance between Tycho and Oliver wasn't based on autobiographical experience, but I did use the backdrop of the summer camp in Knoxville, Tennessee that I'd been to and my travels to Norway. I started, tried, failed, started again, and, after a while, there was a manuscript that my Dutch publisher was willing to publish. Although I barely had a say in how the story unfolded out of me, I knew one thing: even though at the end they would be separated by distance and time, the protagonists would not be letting each other go. It will come as no surprise, then, that Tycho and Oliver lived on even after I finished the book. In time I went on to write another two books about them: the sequel *Our Third Body*, published in 2006, about Tycho going off to college after returning from Norway, and the prequel *Oliver*, published in 2015, and set two years before the events of *Bluegrass Love*. I was able to do that because of the boys themselves, but also because of a wonderful gift that I was given: to this day, Tycho and Oliver continue to appear in the messages I receive from readers. *The Days of Bluegrass Love* and those emails changed my life. I came to understand that a book is nothing if there is no one out there on the other side—the young people who are willing to make it into *their* book. One reader wrote that he had used it to confess his love to his best friend; another said he'd read it a total of seventeen times; yet another addressed his letters not to me but to Tycho. I learned from them and others that the purpose of a book is to pass on a fever—if only to a handful of others. That's why I'm profoundly grateful to my European publishers and readership for the way they made room in their lives for Tycho and Oliver back then. And now, twenty-two years after Tycho and Oliver got their start, I'd like to offer my warmest thanks to my American publisher, Arthur Levine, my brilliant editor, Nick Thomas, my

brilliant translator, Emma Rault, and everyone at
Levine Querido for allowing the fever that every bluegrass love can be to keep on burning.

Edward van de Vendel

ABOUT THE AUTHOR

Edward van de Vendel has been a school principal, founder, and teacher. He has won many of the highest prizes for children's literature in the Netherlands, including the Golden Kiss Award (for best young adult fiction) for *The Days of Bluegrass Love* and its two sequels, and has been nominated four times for the international Astrid Lindgren Memorial Award. He lives in Amersfoort, and travels widely.

ABOUT THE TRANSLATOR

Emma Rault is a writer of creative non-fiction and an award-winning translator from German and Dutch. She lives in Los Angeles.

SOME NOTES ON THIS BOOK'S PRODUCTION

The art for the cover was created by Celina Pereira by processing images with Adobe CS Photoshop and using brush tools to illustrate the two figures perched in the yellow circle. The type treatment was created by hand with marker on paper. The hand-drawn type was then scanned into the computer, cleaned up, and incorporated into the final composition. The text was set by Westchester Publishing Services, in Danbury, CT, in Trump Mediaeval, an old-style serif designed by Georg Trump for Linotype in 1954. The mediaeval name refers to the German typographical term for roman typefaces dark in color, like the old style Venetian typefaces. The display was set in Dear Joe Four, a typeface made around 2005 by JOEBOB Graphics in the Netherlands, created to evoke designer Jeroen van der Ham's handwriting at the time. The book was printed on FSC™-certified 98gsm UPM woodfree paper and bound in China.

Production was supervised by Leslie Cohen
and Freesia Blizard
Book jacket, case, and interiors
designed by Semadar Megged
Edited by Nick Thomas

LEVINE QUERIDO